# The Landscaper's Wife

*The Continuing Love Story of*

*Divided Mountain*

## Annette Stephenson

# Acknowledgments

*All my books are inspired by my loving husband. He is a gifted artist, painting beautiful landscapes that made me fall in love with him. Forty years together giving me three children and everything I need to feel loved. Thank you my love for all you do to keep me in love with you. We were just teenagers when we met, but in my heart I knew you were the one for me. Divided Mountain and The Landscaper's Wife are dedicated to you with all my love.*

*To my children Oliver, Jacob, Kamara. It has been an honor to be your mother and to love you.*

*I am grateful for my piano and the gift of music.*

# Prologue

Katharine Victoria Carrington. The name that was given to her by her loving husband Garrett, sounded beautiful falling from her lips. Her years of despair and loss were behind her. In Garrett's arms she felt safe, never imagining the boy she saw sitting alone at a garden party would be the one who would pledge his love to her. Garrett thought in his mind that Kate was lovely, that she could be someone he could give his love to. Standing next to her husband was Callen, the younger brother of Garrett. Kate stood there with the brothers and knew forgiveness had taken place between the divided mountain that was still beautiful despite what it had been through. She smiled as she drifted back to the time when her love for the brothers was new. She seen the man who was to become her new brother in law. She was happy that he appeared on that special day. Callen walked slowly using his cane to support the bones that were nearly crushed during his horrific motorcycle accident. He had scars that marked its damage. He learned so much since the day he almost lost his life. He was grateful to the couple who stayed with him until he was able to get help. Callen reflected on so much while he was away before coming to Kate and Garrett's wedding. He knew he took his father for granted. While he was away, it was not important to him to mend their relationship. What if he lost it all because of his selfishness? Did he love his brother deep in his heart? What was Garrett thinking when he saw his brother standing there in the shadow of the sunlight? Garrett thought he was dreaming. This couldn't be his brother. Running closer to the man with the cane by his side, he wanted to collapse from the shock of seeing him.

When Callen was a little boy, he was used to being called Brother. It was an endearing way to address his best friend growing up. As an adult, Garrett again called him by that endearing name. This was in relation to the years they spent getting close until the teenage years caused changes that were destined to come. It was Garrett who received his wish to have Kate as his wife. And it was his dream come true to have Callen there to stand beside him. The smile never left Garrett's face as he held Kate's hand, ready to take their vows. There in front of close friends and parents, Maddy, Charles and Mary, they became Man and Wife. As Garrett kissed his new bride, Callen noticed how beautiful she was. Garrett turned to welcome an embrace between brothers who used to be the...

Divided Mountain.

# Chapter 1

At the conclusion of the ceremony, Mary ran over to hold her son she hadn't seen for what seemed like a lifetime. Holding him, she was thankful her family could adjust after being far apart emotionally. Charles wasn't reluctant to approach his son even though they had words before he left. Callen had a smile on his face upon seeing his father. It didn't matter that he needed help walking. He saw past the pain of his goodbye, knowing in some way he hurt his parents and would be forgiven. But that didn't matter. His time away in Florida gave him the opportunity to think about where his life was going. He could see he was on a dangerous path and could have lost the ones he truly loved. Sitting in his apartment back East, Callen looked deeply at his scars, the damage to his leg and broken friendships. In private, he hated what he had done to himself. He would look at his face in the mirror and cry from the pain and trauma he went through. The nightmares from the crash left him riddled with anxiety. Having to leave that note when he left, hurt him inside. He knew no other way to get closure on his father's conversation with him. He stroked his skin, seeing the scars from his surgery wishing he could go back in time and fix what went wrong. Maybe there was a reason he didn't die. He had a second chance to have a fulfilling life, even if it wasn't with Kate. In Florida, he kept to himself, hobbling near the seawall at the beach. It was a nuisance to walk with a cane that young. He had plans to be an attorney, to make money, and enjoy time on the beach with his friends. He remembered a time when he used to play volleyball with David and his friends. Those days seemed far behind him.

Kate and Garrett were greeting their guests as Callen observed their happiness. He wanted to catch up with his parents later but needed to reconnect with Garrett for a moment. He didn't want to steal their time on that day. He just wanted to be near the man who became what he wanted all because of Kate.

"Hey, man you did it. Congratulations," Callen said.

"Thank you, Brother. What a surprise! You had me tearing up. I thought I wasn't going to get through my vows."

"Yeah, well, I had a lot to think about while I was away. I'm glad I was able to get here. We can talk about us later. I want you to have your day. Kate looks beautiful."

"I never thought this day would get here. It all came together when you arrived. Right now, I'm so glad you are alive."

"I know. There are so many things I want to do in my life. It felt good to see Mom and Dad."

"How long can you stay? I mean, when are you going back to Florida?"

"I'm not. I've decided to move back to Santa Barbara. David is engaged and he has been spending time with his fiancé's family."

"I'm happy you're coming back."

"I'm going to ask Dad if I can stay with them. I feel like I have to start over. I just want to say Garrett, I'm glad you are in my life. Thank you."

"Hey, we have more good times ahead. You need to say hello to Kate. She'd love to see you."

"I'll wait. I don't know what I'd say to her."

"Say anything to her. She is very glad you're here. You're her brother in law. We're a family."

"I'll try to get the chance to talk to her."

"I better get back to the guests before we serve dinner."

As Garrett turned to walk to Kate, he heard Callen call out.

"Garrett, I'm glad you're my brother."

"Yeah, me too. Try to find Sam. He really missed you."

Callen talked to many of the guests that knew him. Some asked why he left but he wouldn't reveal anything. He noticed a plaque near a tree where Garrett was honored for his work in developing the new park he designed. He also saw Kate and Garrett's initials carved on a tree. Across the way he saw his younger brother running toward him.

"Callen!" Sam shouted.

"Hey, Sam. Wow, have you gotten taller?"

"Nah, I'm still a little kid."

"No, you're growing into a young man. How have you been?"

"Missing you. Don't ever leave again, okay?"

"I won't. I'm staying."

"Yeah! Mom still has your bedroom. You can come home now."

"I'll talk to her about that."

"Why do you still have that cane? Are you feeling better?"

"Yes but I still need help walking."

"I miss hanging out with you. I can't wait for you to come home."

"I missed you Sam."

As Callen gazed at the beautiful wedding, he was glad he worked so hard to make it on time. Even the landscape held an aura. He could see the world of natural things through his brother's eyes. It was breathtaking as he watched how the park came to life as guests roamed the grounds. All that time Callen had believed that money, career, and success were the elements of true happiness when Garrett found happiness in his heart. Kate brought out the best in him, giving him something he could broaden out with, his talent for gardens and landscapes. Callen now wanted to be in love, but he felt too broken to think it could happen to him.

As everyone was seated for dinner, Garrett wanted to acknowledge his brother for being at his wedding.

"I want to say how much I appreciate Callen for being here to complete our new family. Thank you my brother. You have been everything to me and a big part of my life."

He was grateful to be in this family. He knew, however, he needed to work on feeling closer to Charles. That would require speaking with him to gain some solace.

Callen was precocious and skilled mathematically. He decided to make changes to his career, no longer wanting to be an attorney. While he was in Florida, he considered becoming a math teacher. Even though it was out of his element, he felt it was time to change things up. He was feeling good about his decision.

As the evening was winding down and the guests were saying goodbye, Callen wanted to talk to his father. All his adult life he had asked his father for help with loans and getting on his feet. He wanted to connect with him in a way that was positive. He had been through a lot and asking his father's permission to come back home was a fear he had to face. Charles was a father who deserved the love and respect his children gave him even if they were grown adults. For now, Callen was staying at a hotel. He only had a few bags and his personal things with him. After the accident, he had to give up his love of riding motorcycles. He didn't know how his father felt after their falling out. Charles looked older to him, as if he had been through the pain of knowing his son left. Was Charles saddened from the way Callen said goodbye, by leaving a note? Callen didn't want to further the grief any more than he already created. He'd seen Mary getting her clutch bag as Charles led her to their car. This was Callen's opportunity to let go of the fear.

"Dad, can I talk to you?"

"Yes, Son."

"Excuse us, Mom," Callen politely said.

"Dad I wanted to tell you that I'm sorry for how we parted. I've had a lot to think about while I was gone. I needed to heal and get my life together. I'm moving back to Santa Barbara. I'm staying at a local hotel. Can I come stay at home for a while? I know it's last minute, but I think we can get back to us being Father and Son again."

"Callen, I would like to know what has been going on. I have so many questions. But this is not the place to discuss these issues. You can stay at home. We can get your bags."

"Thank you Dad." He limped toward his mother.

"Oh, Callen," Charles added.

"Yes."

"Welcome home, Son."

He just smiled. His mother put her arm in his as they walked toward the car. That day was a special one for the family. The had been through so much. Not just the fear that he could have died, but it was an emotional loss they felt...until that day.

# Chapter 2

Kate had been spending time writing after finishing school. She took a story writing class to help her gain skills in composition. All those years of writing short stories and poems paid off. Her talent enabled her to easily pen her thoughts and heartfelt emotions. Garrett enjoyed watching her at her typewriter. He would sneak around her desk trying to discover a new story written yet never published. He would sit by the fireplace, read her manuscripts, and rough drafts, fascinated by the fiction and depth she put into her scripts. Of course, Kate did not want anyone to read her projects until her editor combed through them. He wasn't reading them to critique her; Garrett loved his wife's work. When he would come home, he loved to hear the tapping of her typewriter because it meant she was expressing herself. Even though Kate spent time writing, she managed to make her house a warm and inviting home.

"Hey Kate, I'm home. Are you on the keys again?"

"Yes. Now be quiet. I'm in the middle of a good part."

"Hope it's as romantic as yesterday's," he hugged her from behind. "I'm going to work on the front door hardware before supper."

Garrett bought a house shortly after their marriage. It was a fixer that Garrett remodeled and landscaped for Kate. They couldn't build the cabin she wanted in Santa Barbara. Settling on an old home outside of the city limits, Kate could have the privacy she wanted with her husband. She loved the trees. Garrett made sure he planted her favorites around the sides of their property. She had a border of varied flowers that awakened in Springtime. Florals of pink, violet, and yellow would shine like a rainbow touching the ground. She always wanted a fireplace in her living room and with help from Garrett's friends, he made it happen. Hardwoods covered the floors with a deep rich color and strong wood grain. A hammock was set up in the backyard between two trees for those cozy times that they wanted to cuddle, or when Kate wanted to nap outside. There was a Koi pond with a fountain that would light up at night. Around the back, they cultivated a spot for a vegetable and herb garden. She had a picture in her mind before she was engaged to Garrett. After observing the beautiful projects he worked on, it came to her. It was her dream to make his blue-prints come to life. She would never want to leave. This was where they would have their children, grandchildren, and family gatherings.

Garrett began working full time on other landscapes. Life was good for the couple who looked forward to more years of making memories together.

Kate's mother, Maddy, gave her Karen's trunk with all the keepsakes she left behind. Maddy had been taking care of the house since her sister passed away. She never touched the décor, leaving everything as Karen left it. When Kate and Garrett came over to visit, they would reminisce about all of the good times they experienced within those walls.

Maddy could never imagine selling Karen's house. She planned to keep it in her family for generations. At times, she would kneel by the tree where her sister's ashes were spread and cry, missing the woman who shaped her life for the better. Karen's bedroom was untouched. Maddy's boys no longer shared a room. What was once Kate's room became an office for Maddy. She tended to the garden with the help of her sons. Adding fresh flowers to the table vase, she kept the sense of calm, as if Karen were still there. Rosy came by occasionally to visit, bringing her cheery disposition to uplift Maddy during those times she missed Karen. That feeling would always be managed but never would go away.

Maddy's focus was making sure to care for her sons. Without a father, they relied on their mother for support and advice. Cody and Chase entered private school. Maddy gave her boys the best opportunity to expand their horizons and choose careers that gave them a good start in life.

With her inheritance, Maddy bought the floral shop she worked in and hired new employees with some experience. She also bought a new van for her deliveries.

Thomas Matthews was a regular customer at the floral shop. He would talk to Maddy as if he were interested in her. She knew he was a good man, but dating was not what she was ready for. He kindly respected that and moved on, no longer pursuing her. That was how Maddy stayed emotionally safe. Pain from previous love made it difficult for her to try a new relationship. The man she loved with her whole heart broke her family. Even after he left and was gone for years, she missed him. She finally got over him and happily went on with her life. There were more important things to work on. When Kate went through her rough teenage years, Maddy knew giving love to her daughter would help pull her through.

Kate blossomed into a beautiful woman who gained her reward just like her mother said.

It was the anniversary of Maddy's first year as owner of the floral shop. Rosy wanted to plan a party to celebrate. Because the community was close to the Parkers, Rosy wanted to include them. She came to visit Maddy at her home.

"Hello!" Rosy called through the front screen door. "Congratulations on your anniversary. You really gave that store a new life. I just love the fountain you put in with the houseplants! When customers come in, they are going to hear and feel your style."

"Thank you Rosy. What did you think of the new name on the door?"

"The Gilded Rose. That is wonderful. How is business?"

"It's going great. Thanks for referring James to come on board. He's a good worker. He's always on time."

"He loves his job. So, how have you been?"

"I'm fine. I finally gave Karen's trunk to Kate. I know she would have wanted her to have it. Something has been on my mind. The boys have been asking about their father lately."

"Oh? Well, it could be because they're growing up. It's normal for children to ask where a missing parent is."

"I know, but it's strange. We never talk about him and then they asked me where he is lives. I just tell them I don't know."

"Have you showed them the pictures of him?"

14

"No. I'm not sure if they are ready for that yet. Kate had resentment for the longest time when he left. She doesn't ask about him anymore."

"Try not to overthink it. Your boys love you and they are so much younger than Kate. Just take it slow."

"I don't even know if he is alive. Our relationship was rocky, but I thought it was good even though he had troubles in his mind. I never knew why he left. He just went away with no warning."

"I'm sorry that happened to your family."

"We've been doing fine on our own without him."

Rosy could see the sadness coming through and wanted to change the subject.

"Let's talk about this party I want to throw for your business."

"Where should we have it?"

"Why not here? Your backyard is beautiful."

"Okay, but just a few guests."

"A few? Maddy, the whole community wants to celebrate!"

"Okay. A little more than a few."

"You got it! Now you promised me lunch."

"I did?" Maddy laughed.

The two women came together for support and Maddy appreciated Rosy listening. The closeness they felt for each other boosted Maddy's positive outlook. Her small community of friends had been her life, giving her what she needed to come back after Karen's death.

Maddy felt whole. Her daughter was married, her sons were growing up right, and she had a successful business. Thinking about Daryl and how curious her sons were about him was a little uncomfortable. She knew she would have to talk about him, but she had to be ready. Until then, she would calm her fears by not thinking about it.

The boys came home and raided the fridge after little league practice.

"Hey, shoes at the front door. Eat your snacks out back."

"Okay, Mom."

"Dinner is at six so don't eat too much. After you are finished with your snack, shower and clothes in the hamper. You smell like sweat and grass!"

"Can we ride bikes first?"

"No, get cleaned up, then homework."

"Aw, Mom!"

"They are sure growing fast," Rosy observed.

"Yes and teenage years are coming."

"You're ready for that."

"It was hard enough going through that with Kate. I hope you're right."

After Rosy left Maddy's house, Maddy searched her closet to retrieve something she kept concealed. Reaching up to the top shelf, she grabbed an envelope and opened it again. She hadn't looked at it since she received it years before in New York. Maddy didn't even show it to Karen. Inside was the letter from Daryl. The return address was Anonymous. She guessed he didn't want the children to know he tried to contact Maddy. There was a photograph of him with his new wife and baby. Maddy never wanted anyone to know that he wrote her. The day she received it; her tears ran seeing him with his new family.

The letter read:

*Madeline,*

*I wanted to write you even though I know you will never forgive me for abandoning you and the kids. I went to see a psychiatrist a few months after I left. I needed to get help and I was feeling better after treatment. I wanted to come back, but I knew you were too hurt to let me back into your life. I had to move on and start over. I was alone and felt like I was going to lose my mind without someone to love me. I had no family, and all my friends left me. I wanted to come to you, but the rejection was too much for me to bear. Maybe I was misjudging you and should have given you a chance to forgive me. I became afraid and stayed away. I met someone at my new job, and we are very happy. She gave me a son. His name is Connor. He's very beautiful, like his mother.*

*I have good and bad days. There are times when I don't want to take medication, but Annie helps me through it. How are you? Have you met someone new? How are my children? I don't want to hurt them, so please don't share this with them. I know I was a loser for a father. I want to be forgiven, but if you feel you can't do that, it is okay. I just wanted you to know I still love Chase, Cody, and Katharine. In my heart I love you too because you are their mother. The address inside the letter is my new place of residence. If you want to, you can write me back. I told my wife I was writing you. Please let me know how the children are. Best Wishes, Daryl Parker*

Her conscience made her feel guilty for not sharing this with her children. At the time, she was too distraught to read it to them. She had just gotten her life back and then her sons wanted to know about him. Maddy put the envelope back, hiding it away. She thought about what Rosy said, ease into telling them. Maddy would know when the time was right. For the time, she had to put it to rest.

# Chapter 3

Garrett had made plans to visit his brother who was adapting to living with his parents again. He was busy working on his landscape projects but needed to take the time to see him.

Callen didn't want to live with his parents. He was looking for work while applying for schooling to become a math teacher. Callen didn't want to talk to his father about his latest career choice. He was worried he would try to talk him out of it. He knew he would have to study for years to fulfill his goal. It would be good for him to venture into a new field on his own.

Garrett didn't know about Callen's plans either. That day, he wanted to be sure his brother was okay.

"Hey, Garrett. Come in. How's married life?"

"Good, very good. I've been working on the house. Kate's been writing her books. She's hesitating to get them published, but I think she will."

"That's great! It's good to see you. Let's go out to the backyard."

"Mom's famous iced tea?"

"You know it. So what's on your mind?" Callen asked.

"I wanted to catch up on how you're doing. What made you decide to move back?"

"I needed a change. I felt alone and then I had to see a doctor."

"Doctor? About what?"

"I don't know if I want to talk about it."

"You know you can trust me Callen. What is it?"

"I was diagnosed with Post-Traumatic Stress Disorder, or they call it, PTSD."

"How did you get that?"

"It's a mental trauma thing. I have been having nightmares and not sleeping. It's from the accident. I had to see the therapist to talk it out. I moved back home to get away. I felt miserable in Florida."

"Oh Callen, I'm sorry. So, what are you going to do now? Do the parents know?"

"No. I want to talk to Dad about the last time we talked but I haven't gotten the courage up yet. I'm not sure how they will take the news that I'm screwed up."

"I wouldn't say that. You went and got help. That's a good step in the right direction."

"Do you want to know what made me want to mend things with you?" he rubbed his hand through his hair.

"That's over. I'm just glad you're here."

"I know you won't believe this, but I've always wanted to be like you."

"You told me one time you were jealous of me. You don't have to feel that way."

20

"What I was going through wasn't your fault. You were in the spotlight, and it felt lonely being outside that light."

"I don't let that hurt me anymore. Yes, I was hurt. But I still had hope we would get it together."

"I pulled us apart. I knew I would never get what you earned. I thought about how much I wanted to be a father someday. I could teach my kids to be themselves, communicate and love them, just be there. I felt lost not having Dad on my side."

"It was a big loss for all of us. Tell me what you want to do."

"I'm going to enroll at the university to be a math teacher."

"If this is what is going to make you happy, I'd go for it."

"My concentration is off so I hope the doctor can help me deal with these thoughts I have. Sometimes it's a noise or the sound of a motorcycle on the road. It freaks me out. Things are better, but I still struggle."

"I'm sure they can help. I'm here if you need me."

"I know. I'm sorry Garrett for being apart. If I could, I would go back and..."

"Hey, it's okay. All is forgiven. I want you to know how much I am glad you didn't die that day. I cried at night thinking about how you came so close to death. Brother, here you are. You are taking control of your life."

"I'm trying. I look at my scars and hate how hard it is to walk normally. It's a constant reminder of who I was. I never want to take you for granted again."

"You won't."

"Tell Kate hello for me. I should see her and congratulate her."

"She understands. I won't tell her about your issues."

"I appreciate that."

The brothers were mending. It was slow but Callen had lost himself in the mix of all the emotions he was going through. He felt he had to cross off some of the things he needed to do to gain control again. The most important was to let his father know what caused his frustration. Charles had not made the first move to get involved in his returning son's life. He hadn't even asked him how things were. Callen didn't care about who started the conversation. He wanted to end the constant fight he was battling in his head. He wasn't sure if his dad was ready for that. The night terrors were bad while in Florida. David knew his friend needed help and after getting engaged, he suggested he move back home to get some support. Callen's panic attacks were debilitating, and it made it difficult for him to keep his job. He received great care, but he knew moving back would help him with the healing process. After Callen moved back, his mother approached him with a cup of coffee.

"Callen, dear. It's so good to have you back."

"Thanks, Mom. How are you?"

"I should be asking you that question? Are you okay, Son?"

"Yeah, I'm fine. I missed my family."

"I'm not sure if you want to talk about it, but why are you home?" She leaned in, "I thought you liked living in Florida."

"I did, but David got engaged and I just missed home."

"I'm happy for David. You know Callen, your father worried about you. You just left and never got in touch with us."

"I know and I'm sorry for that."

"That's why I asked if you were okay. If you ever need anything, I'm here. Give your father a chance to hear you. Don't give up on him."

"I won't."

"Good. I know you'll do the right thing."

Mary was a mother who wanted to fix all the issues the family went through. It wasn't in her to give up. She sensed Callen was home for more reasons than he revealed. She had a feeling he was holding back. She was also a little afraid to find out why. Callen had been more quiet than she was used to. She was happy that he was safe. After everything they had been through, that was relieving.

Callen had taken some time to get to know Sam. All the years of ignoring his brothers was wearing on him. He felt guilty for all those times Sam wanted to be with him, and he pushed him aside. Callen was young and it wasn't too late for Sam to connect with his brother again.

"Do you want to throw the ball around?"

"Sure. Can I get my mitt?" asked Sam.

23

"Yep, go get it."

Sam was excited to have time with Callen. He was impressionable and had learned to live around his family with all they went through. Sam spoke many times about wanting to be like Garrett. Trying to get close to Callen was something he gave up on. But he saw a difference in his brother that day. Sam was almost eleven and a young boy like him needed a good influence to help him project who he would be like.

Callen tossed the ball at a short distance a few times while leaning against the cane.

"Can you try to throw the ball to me without your cane?" Sam asked.

"I don't think I can, buddy. My knee is still weak."

"Can you try?"

Callen saw the plea in his brother's eyes. He didn't like the weakness he felt without it. It had been a part of him for a while.

"Alright, Sam. I'll try it."

Callen reluctantly tried to let it go. The weakness had him falling to the ground.

"Callen!" Sam shouted as he ran to his side.

"It's okay, Sam."

"Let me help you."

"I can do it." Callen got up and walked away.

"Where are you going?"

24

"I think I'm done for the day. Sorry, Sam."

He wouldn't look back. Sam's disappointment was too hard to see. It broke Callen's heart to let him down. Sam decided to follow Callen.

"Callen, I know you tried. I'm not a little kid anymore. I know you hate that cane. I do too. I want to be your friend. I'm sorry I asked you to drop the cane."

"Hey, hey. Don't say that. You did nothing wrong. I've had a lot of surgeries and it gives me some trouble at times. I will get better in time. We both just have to be patient. Can you do that for me, buddy?"

"I can."

"Good boy! Let me rest up and we'll finish our game, okay?"

"Okay."

Callen's heart was changing for the better. He didn't want Sam to end up like him. His weak leg reminded him of that. Sam deserved a brother who could help him grow into manhood with the proper values. Callen wanted to give him that. He did try to sacrifice the use of his cane to play with him and the smile on Sam's face left Callen feeling like they made a new start.

Charles no longer put his work before his family. After his heart attack, he slowed down. He had the roof repaired, he took Mary on a cruise, and officially retired. Sitting in his office, he studied the photos of his children on the bookshelf. He looked out the window and noticed Callen and Sam. He wanted to be there for his sons, but he was holding back. He wasn't sure why. Callen was alive and he was home. While his son was in Florida, Charles thought about the night Callen had his accident. At first, he felt guilty for not forcing his son to stay home that night. He blamed himself and it affected his relationship with Mary. Watching Callen, he looked at him with the cane and hoped his son could walk normally again. He still nursed his hurt feelings from the night before Callen left. He would think, "What if he died and we never came together?" Charles had those private moments where he cried for Callen. He held it in for so long until he read the note Callen left. He thought that Mary and his family could have lost the both of them. They were supposed to be a family; love had gathered them through other hard times.

"Charles, what you are doing in here, love?" Mary asked.

"Just looking at all of these old photographs of our family and thinking about Callen. I was watching him out there with Sam. I'm grateful he's alive."

"I know it was hard for you to deal with the distance you two had. What's wrong, dear? Why can't you talk to him?"

"How do I make up for all those years I wasn't there? I took it for granted and then I had the heart attack. I could have lost it all."

"But you didn't. We are here together. You will know when to be there for him. He's different, I think he's better."

"I can see that. I think there's more to his story than he's letting on."

"You may be right. He doesn't need saving; he needs to heal."

Mary kissed Charles and left the room. He was waiting for Callen but that wasn't what was best. Waiting would get them nowhere. It shouldn't be about who was going to make the first move. It should be about giving love to a son who needed it. He was reminded of his grandfather's words, "Communication is the responsible thing to do when love is involved."

It was sad that he didn't live by those words when it came to Callen.

That evening, David had called Callen. It had been a few weeks since they last talked.

"Callen, I thought I'd call and see how you're doing."

"I'm good. Are you making wedding plans?"

"Well, that's why I was calling. Are you going to be here for the wedding?"

"I want to come but I'm not sure it's the right time."

"Are you still having the nightmares? You scared me the last time you were here. Is that why you don't think you can make it?"

"We talked about this when I got on that plane. I told you I may never come back to Florida."

"It's my wedding, Callen. You're my best friend. I really thought you would be there to make it complete."

"Let me get on my feet first. I know it's a lot to ask but can I just some have time to get better? Because of how I've been feeling, you wouldn't want me there."

"I'm not sure what to say, Cal. It won't be the same without you there."

"Things have changed, David. I can't run anymore or ride a motorcycle again. I can't even play with Sam without this stupid cane. I don't want to be pressured to do something I'm not ready for."

"Okay, don't come. Get well first. I hope your disability doesn't change our friendship. I can't imagine my life without you in it."

"I know. This is going to take more time than I want. I wish I could be there."

"Take care, man."

Callen hung up the phone. He had both hands on his head, feeling tortured by his disorder. He had to believe that he would get control back one day. What was it that was going to change his view on normalcy? It was going to take work and that meant going back to physical therapy and getting control of his mental health. He thought back to when the fear came into his life.

David and Callen had planned a trip with friends to ride ATV's. David's uncle had some land where they could ride. It was an open area that had trails wide enough for the vehicles. Callen had a brace on his leg to help with the tension. They all rode there for the day. There were about six vehicles with two on each one to ride. Callen heard the revving of the engines, and his heart was pounding fast. He didn't know what his body was going through. Sitting behind David, Callen began to shake. As they began to ride with the others, Callen shouted, "Stop! Stop now!"

David helped Callen off and saw his friend on the ground crying and fearful. David had his uncle drive them to the house to help him calm down. Callen was bombarded with nightmares several times a week and he was urged to get help. Callen talked to his doctor and started treatment to control the anxiety. He became distant and didn't want to socialize with his friends. That was when he made the decision to return to California.

Callen admitted to himself that he was feeling better in a familiar place with his family. He didn't want to feel pathetic and lost in the world. He knew a friend who worked at the university that may be able to get him an internship and help him get enrolled. He had to start somewhere.

Charles readied himself to talk to Callen.

"Hi, Son. Do you think we can take some time to talk? We haven't spoken much since you've been back."

"I would like that. I have some other things I'm trying to get done first. Can I let you know?"

"Yeah, sure. Anytime."

"Thanks, Dad."

Callen thought he was going into the unknown accepting his father's invitation. He didn't want to reveal how much stress he was experiencing. He wasn't sure how Charles would handle it. He admired his father's courage to work things out, but he wasn't ready. Having PTSD was embarrassing to admit. It made him feel weak and insignificant. He was afraid Charles may bring up any weaknesses he had seen in him. Callen was prepared to be grilled about the mistakes he made and that made him feel insecure. For the longest time Callen's mind replayed the accident with all of its noises and pain. His thoughts did not get better. His recovery was grueling, and he became afraid when the doctor told him he would lose his leg if the surgeries didn't take.

Callen laid in bed looking at the patterns on the ceiling. His mind would not let him sleep. He thought about Kate and what she did for him. All his life he felt alone, and everything felt easier when Kate showed an interest in him. It all fell to pieces when she no longer cared about him romantically. Callen had to take the blame. He knew it wasn't Kate's fault. He let the excitement of Florida create a distance that led to his loss. He respected her as a married woman and wanted to have a different relationship with her. She was strong. He needed her around to gain strength. Callen recalled the day Kate came to the hospital to visit. It was hard to hear between her tears that it was her fault. He had to amend that thought. He hoped Kate wasn't still holding on to the guilt. He admitted to himself that he wasn't in love with her but wanted to be. He tried to be a devoted boyfriend; he knew something else prevented that from happening. Callen kept asking himself why, questioning every thought of doubt deep within. In his mind he tortured himself, 'what have I done?' He so desperately wanted to go back to who he was. That would take time and effort on his part. But most of all, it would take guts to talk to Charles. He really wanted that bond back. It would be worth it.

# Chapter 4

Kate was taking a break from writing to help Garrett with some small landscaping projects. She wanted to spend more time with him. She remembered those times when she and Garrett used to go to work helping the community with their backyard designs. She still had the book Garrett gave her on plants and botany. It was a wonderful memory for a couple whose love grew among the trees. Kate now wanted to make new memories for her and her husband. She often thought about being a mother. She went to a few baby showers Rosy had for some of her friends and felt empty in her heart wanting a child of her own. She didn't know how Garrett would feel if she brought up the subject. Did he ever think about being a dad? Would he want a child? Because everything was going so well, she was nervous to bring it up. She would find the right time to talk about the idea and see where it would lead them.

Garrett started a big job on a historically restored home. The landscape was in terrible shape with overgrown Ivy and dead bushes. Some of the trees were diseased and had to be cut down. Garrett preferred not to destroy any foliage, giving the plants a chance to thrive. It was his nurturing spirit that prompted calls for him to bring spaces to life again. His talent was deepened by the love Kate had for her dear landscaper. Every day she fell deeper in love seeing another garden he designed. He used to go around town looking for yards in need. Garrett would meet the owners of the home and get to know them. If they were interested, he would grab his sketch pad from the truck and draw out a design in front of them that would enhance the home's architecture. Kate was glowing as she watched her husband create. The way he cared for people warmed her heart, thinking how he would love his own children. On one job, she stood back watching her husband solving a problem and laughing with clients. He was in a happy place. The thought of being a landscaper's wife was no longer a dream for Kate. She loved being a wife and now her desire to be a mom was growing.

Kate was home preparing dinner. She looked at her office and stared at her typewriter. She hadn't written anything for a few days. She was too busy thinking about how she was going to talk to Garrett. Her husband would be coming home soon. She always loved to greet him with a good meal and the fireplace ready for a cool evening. She smiled when he came home, smelling of wood and scented with soil. Dirty clothes made her happy since that meant he worked hard doing what he loved. He always greeted her with a kiss and an 'I love you.' He was living the good life with Kate. Each day he came home, he was in a place where love lived. She made everything good for Garrett. Occasionally she would be in the kitchen, and he would surprise her with a hug around her waist, kissing her on the cheek. No woman could feel more loved.

"Something smells good. How was your day, love?" Garrett asked.

"It was good. I didn't write anything, but I hope you're hungry. I made chicken soup."

"I love your soups. Let me clean up and I'll be there to sit with you."

She set the table, put the hot bread in a basket, and covered it with a small towel. She made some homemade jam to go with their meal. Cold butter rested in a dish nearby, he liked it cold. By the back door, she could see pieces of bark, moss, and soil on the floor. She cared little about the mess he left. He was a gifted landscaper and the love of her life. This was where she wanted to be. She shared everything with her Garrett.

"What a nice meal to come home to. Why didn't you write today?"

"I did some laundry and wanted to talk to you about something."

"Everything alright?"

"Oh, everything is fine. Maybe we can talk about it after dinner."

"You know we can talk about anything together. If it's on your mind, let's discuss it."

Kate took a breath. She was quiet for a moment.

"Honey, what is it?" Garrett begged.

"Well, I've been thinking about a subject I'm not sure you are ready for."

"What is the subject?"

"A baby. I want to have a baby with you."

Garrett slowly smiled at Kate and took her hand. Kate was relieved that Garrett was not disappointed in her request.

"A baby? I never thought we would talk about kids until later. Are you sure you are ready for that?"

"I think I am. I've been thinking about it for a while. I couldn't concentrate on writing until we talked about it. I wanted to know your thoughts."

"Love, you know I would love to have a baby with you."

"Do you want to think about it or talk about it?"

"Think about it."

"Okay."

"I love you Kate. If we do have a baby, I hope we have a daughter that looks just like you."

"We'll probably have a son who brings more dirt in the house than you."

"We will love them just like I love you."

Every night after dinner Kate and Garrett would sit on the porch swing in their backyard. Warm Earl Grey tea and her in his arms was a beautiful picture of this couple and their love.

Maddy was busy at the floral shop with weddings and special occasions. She hadn't talked to Kate in a few weeks. She put it on her list to make sure to call her later. Maddy thought about Daryl again, wondering how she was going to approach her boys about the questions they had about the father that abandoned them. The letter she read gave her some hope he changed and wanted to rectify his relationships. She still wasn't trusting even after reading what he sent. She would not answer him back. He never wrote again. She tried for so long not to think about the first man she ever loved even after he left. She wanted to tell Kate about it many times, but she didn't want to aggravate her further. She wondered about the right time to reveal it and let her children know more about Daryl Parker.

"Kate, I'm sorry I haven't called. The shop has been busy."

"Oh, it's okay. I went on some jobs with Garrett, and I stopped writing for a few days."

"That's not like you to stop writing. Running out of ideas for your books?"

"No, I talked to Garrett about having a baby."

"Kate, you want to make me a grandma? Wow, are you two thinking about it?"

"Yes. I'm giving him some space."

"You'll make a great mom. You learned from the best," Maddy smiled.

"I sure did."

"Kate, let's get together soon."

"I'd like that. Next week is a good time."

Kate always confided in Maddy. She built trust in her. When Kate attempted to ruin her own life with rebellion, Maddy never reacted in a negative way. She was a good mother. She had to make a crucial decision to tell her children about their father. Maddy would do what was best for them. For now, Daryl was not in her life, and nothing should complicate what she built with her kids.

Maddy knew what Kate was going through. She lost her own father at a very young age. Her mother never remarried. Michelle did what she could to be sure her girls were happy without the father they loved. Maddy and Karen were raised by their grandmothers who helped Michelle carry the weight of being a responsible parent. Their mother would cry sometimes missing Scott. She didn't want to settle on a husband just to make a complete family. Together they were a family, even if Scott wasn't there.

Maddy felt like she was silently hurting her children by not telling them their father got in touch with her. Would Kate be interested in knowing he wrote? How would that make her feel? Maddy had to think it through, carefully explaining how she wanted to protect them in case he returned.

While alive, Karen loved the elegant things in life. She lived a blessed lifestyle with Michael, had a career as a high school teacher, and most of all she had her sister. Maddy was the opposite. She did not go to college. She moved out at seventeen, living with her friend's family. She was dating Daryl at the time and her mother did not agree. At the age of eighteen, Maddy married Daryl. Karen and Michael reservedly stood by her side. A courthouse wedding was not what Maddy expected but at the time she thought marrying Daryl would help her situation. After the wedding, they moved into an apartment complex where Maddy managed the apartments. She was good at her job, making sure the complex was running smoothly. Daryl was having a hard time staying at a job. He quit many times and could not keep enough income in the family. There were times he wouldn't come home until late in the evening. One time he slept in his car after work and came home the next day. The weight of the depression set in, and it affected his marriage. Maddy became pregnant with Kate. It was unexpected news for the struggling young couple. Daryl had times when his stress was too much for him and he emotionally distanced himself from his wife and daughter. After trying to get help, Daryl got a job working at a factory where they would recycle plastics. Cody was born and Maddy felt like a family again. They had many good memories together until Daryl lost the factory job. Maddy was expecting a third baby, a boy they named Chase. It got tougher and Daryl no longer confided in his wife. She couldn't control the sadness he was going through. To her surprise, Daryl left and never returned. It was as if the breath was taken from her. She lost the will to try anymore. Moving out and becoming homeless, Maddy looked into the eyes of her children. With dirty faces and very little possessions, she picked herself up and started to move on. Living in a tiny apartment was her only choice. The manager was having a move in special, no deposit and only half the rent if they signed on that day. It was all the money Maddy had, and they called that place home until they moved to California.

Maddy looked back on her life and observed how her patience brought her to a good place. It was hard but she made it without Daryl. She was honest and true to who she was. She knew what she had to do and even though it wasn't going to be easy, it was the right thing. She would have the right words to say to ease her children into the reasons why. If the outcome was upsetting, she knew she did her best. So just like her mother, Maddy didn't need to have a man around to feel complete. She was good on her own.

# Chapter 5

Callen had been spending time with his mentor at the University of California in Santa Barbara. He was an intern, sitting in on some classes watching teachers shape young minds. His forte was mathematics. Amazingly, Callen was talented in that field. He used to work at a hotel as a CPA and bookkeeper. He had dreams to be a tax attorney, but he thought more about becoming a teacher. Matt Abbott was an experienced math teacher who specialized in Algebra, Trigonometry and Calculus. This was someone Callen could really learn from. He loved to be challenged and wasn't afraid of hard work.

"Have you enrolled yet?" Matt asked.

"No. I got a grant for tuition, but I wasn't sure when to start."

"The next scheduled enrollment, I would give it some thought. You're good, very good. You already have it in you, use it to help your studies."

"Okay, I'll do it. I realize it will take hard work."

"It will take more than that. Commit yourself, turn in your assignments and take time to study."

"I understand. Thank you, Matt."

Callen left that meeting feeling confident. Keeping himself distracted helped curb his anxiety. Spending a few hours as an observer gave Callen the will to try to get his life back. He left the classroom, and he would return another day to be coached by Matt. On the way out, he bumped into someone.

"Oh, I'm sorry. Are you alright?" Callen asked.

"Yeah, I think so."

She was a very pretty student named Cassie Adams. In her arms were papers she was carrying to administration.

"Let me help you pick these up." Callen bent on one knee.

"Thank you. I've never seen you here at school before. Are you a new student?"

"Yes, well, I will be. I'm enrolling to be a math teacher. I'm an intern with Matt Abbott."

"I know Matt. He's a great teacher. This is my first year as a student. I'm studying to be a history teacher."

"I feel bad I bumped into you. I'm Callen Carrington."

"Cassie Adams. I better get these to the office. It was nice to meet you."

"Bye, Cassie."

Callen watched her leave. It made him smile and he hoped he would see her again. She seemed to not notice the cane he was using. She never even asked about it. That made him feel good about going to this facility.

Kate thought of talking to Callen. She still had a special feeling for the man who was now her family. At her wedding, she noticed that he was different, he seemed quieter. While she was observing him, he looked back at her.

It wasn't romantic. It was a wonderment of where they both were emotionally.

Mid-morning Kate was at home. As she came into the living room, her eyes scanned over the pictures of Callen and Garrett. She had a part in bringing the two back together. She was thinking that maybe she should pay Callen a visit and see how he really was. At one time, he confided in her and they briefly had a conversation before he left. That would help Kate feel more comfortable around him. She decided to call on him at his home without notice.

"Kate, what a surprise. What are you doing here?" Callen asked.

"We didn't get a chance to talk at the wedding. I was so happy you came, and I didn't get to tell you that."

"Would you like to come in?"

"Yes, I would. Does your mom have any pie?"

"Sure. Have a seat and I'll get you some."

"Thanks Callen."

"I'm glad I came to your wedding but at first it was a bit of a shock for me," Callen said as he served her.

"I sensed it was overwhelming."

"I needed to fix myself, gather my thoughts and try to make some changes."

"Changes? I think you could have used a break after all that happened since the accident. But I thought you were fine."

41

"I had to have another surgery. After that the world stopped and I was incapacitated again."

"Were you not able to walk, what was it?"

"Physical therapy was not easy, so I quit. I had to get over you. That took some time. When I got the invite to the wedding, I knew I would regret it if I didn't go. I really care about Garrett and Sam. To be honest, I was afraid to see you standing there in your dress."

"As my friend, don't you want me happy?"

"Yes, I do. You got what was best for you. Me, I feel broken."

"No, don't say that. You just need time. I'm happy you are back from Florida. You know, Garrett thinks highly of you as a brother."

"The biggest thing I struggle with is that I can't go back and undo the damage I caused."

"I know how you feel."

"Really? How do you know?"

"I hung out with the wrong crowd as a young girl. My teenage years were sad, and I was angry. I was even arrested for being stupid."

"I didn't know that. I can't imagine you in jail."

"I did nothing wrong; I just hung out with losers. I was in a bad place in my life. It was scary. But when I met your family, I moved on from it. I didn't care how long it took. I had to heal on my own."

"Sometimes I think if I met someone special I would be a better man."

"I believe for some, that is true. It is probably better to know who you want to be first. Don't lose hope if you want to be happy."

"It so strange that you are my family now."

"Well, I wouldn't say strange. Maybe something new," she smiled.

"I don't want to take anything for granted."

"I hope you find happiness where ever you go. I really want that for you. You deserve it," consoled Kate.

"I'm sorry I hurt you Kate. Can you forgive me?"

"Yes, I did. Forgiveness is welcomed in my world. My mother once said to me that I would get my reward in time if I was patient. I'm passing that on to you. You will have yours too."

The two exchanged stories about where they've been in their lives. Callen was like the long lost brother Kate waited for. She knew it was hard for him, but she never judged him. He was human. Kate found a friend in Callen. She felt she was a small support to the Carrington family, and she was going to be there for the ones she loved. Kate was a heroine, but she didn't want to feel that way. What she did for this family was out of love. They were a strong mountain, holding its strength and beauty for all time. Callen was part of that, no matter what he was going through.

After their visit, Callen watched Kate leave. He thought about what she said, and he was taking it to heart. He still wasn't ready to share his anxieties with her. The feelings he was having were now for an adored sister who came to his rescue.

Charles was walking by when he heard their conversation. As he listened from around the corner Charles came to realize that his son was damaged. He felt he was responsible for much of it. If he couldn't reach his son that day, he was going to do everything in his power to get Callen back.

# Chapter 6

Garrett had been working on a project that was owned by a group of people who were professional botanists. They were from Europe and moved to the States to train and mentor those who were skilled in landscaping. Garrett liked being around those who loved the art. He spent time studying tree surgery and plant diseases, so he felt comfortable working alongside other dendrologists. The grounds were about twenty acres filled with varied species. Classes were offered teaching disease prevention, growth, and nutrient enrichment for foliage, flowers, and vegetables. Garrett placed an order for some Bloodgood Japanese Maple trees that would brighten up the area.

"Garrett, it seems we ordered one too many of the Japanese Maple for this space. Should we return it?" asked one of the plantsmen.

"No, I'll take it. I know the perfect place for it."

"Should we load it on your truck?"

"Please. Make sure to secure it tightly."

Garrett thought about the conversation he had with Kate about starting a family. The tree reminded him of her. Since they first met, she mentioned how she loved Maples. Garrett wanted to surprise his wife.

He pulled into the driveway where Kate could see him. She came outside to see what was in his truck.

"Garrett, what did you bring home?"

"Do you like it?"

"Yes, but why is it here?"

"I thought about what you said, about us starting a family. I think it would be wonderful to have a baby with you. What do you say, are you ready to have a family?"

"Yes, yes, my love. But why is the tree here?" Kate asked.

"I know Karen and Michael would plant a new tree to remember their family. I want to plant this tree for our firstborn."

"I love that. Thank you!"

Kate had to wrap her arms around the man who made a difference in her life. She was looking forward to being a mother. They planted the tree together, putting it in a spot where it would thrive with the others. The beautiful bright colors blew in the wind loving their new home. Nothing could have made Kate happier in that moment.

Maddy contemplated how to reveal Daryl's letter to Kate. Cody was getting older and the questions he had about his father were getting more perplexing. She didn't quite know how to address them. Cody came home from school looking for Maddy. She was upstairs in her office preparing a large order for an event when Cody walked in.

"Mom, are you busy?"

"I can take a break. I have to get this order out before tomorrow. What is it, honey?"

46

"Remember when we talked about my dad the other day? It seemed like you didn't want to talk about it. I just want to know what he was like."

"We haven't talked about him much. I knew the day would come when you would ask me about him."

"Did he die?"

"No, he just left us. I think he was too sad. I tried to help him, but he just couldn't find happiness at home."

"Why would a dad leave his family? Have you ever talked to him?"

"No. He did...no, I never talked to him."

"Can you tell me a little about him, right now?"

"Sure I can."

Maddy went on to tell Cody about the happier times they had as a family so as not to put his father in a bad light. Maddy fostered little resentment over the breakup of her marriage. She never wanted that to reflect on her children. Sitting down as Mother and Son gave Maddy a special time to see her son growing into a young man. Cody had said during this talk, "I would never leave my family." Maddy had hopes her children would learn from her and the love she showed them. She got them off to a good start and could see her love gave them a chance. She was proud of Kate and where she was in her life. After they talked, Cody held her, thanking her for the input he needed. She didn't reveal much about Daryl, just enough to get his interest satisfied. Maddy felt bad that she didn't share the letter he wrote. It was something she felt was just between them. She thought about it and didn't think it was right to keep the secret to herself.

Maddy received a phone call from one of her friends in New York. Josephine was a close friend of Maddy's. She offered a small place in her home for Maddy's family to stay when they were homeless.

"Josephine, it's so good to hear from you. What a surprise."

"I'm glad I called you. I know we haven't spoken in a year. My daughter got married and my grandson had to move back in with me. It's been quite a year. What about you?"

"Kate got married. The boys are growing up so fast. So, what's going on?"

"Maddy, someone came to see me yesterday. I think you want to sit down for this."

"Who came to see you?"

"Daryl came by and asked about you. I told him you moved to California. I didn't tell him your number or address. He wanted me to give him any information about you and the kids. I just couldn't do that."

Maddy felt like she couldn't breathe. She just finished talking to Cody about him and this news was shocking.

"Why is he looking for me?"

"I don't know. He was nice and he looked decent. He was polite and just needed the information."

"The boys have been asking about him. I talked to Cody briefly about him."

"They are getting at that age where they will want to know about him."

"He wrote me a letter and I still haven't told Kate."

"It may be time for you to share that with her."

"I'm not ready yet."

"Maddy, I think Daryl is harmless. I wasn't sure why he came by and wanted to see you. But I think he is alone, maybe his wife isn't with him anymore."

"If he finds me, it won't be a good time. I'm not ready for any of this."

"Well, I'm here if you need me."

"Thank you, Jo."

Maddy didn't want Daryl back in her life. She was getting the feeling that he wanted her back. Was that a definite possibility? It had been years since the letter was sent to her in New York. She was afraid of the reason he wanted to contact her. Could it be for custody of the boys? Did he lose his wife? She had so many questions. Since he didn't know where her address was, she was relieved that he would not find her. Even though Jo had said he was harmless, how would she know that for herself?

Chase and Cody were preparing to go to Summer Camp for eight weeks. This would give Maddy a chance to catch up on some work around the house and have time to herself. She didn't want to talk about Daryl any further with her boys. It was causing her undue stress; afraid he would resurface somehow. Maddy was organizing her office and closet when the phone rang. It was Kate.

"Hi Mom. Did the boys leave yet?"

"No. I'm sorting through some things and packing their bags. They are leaving early next week."

"What are you going to do for those eight weeks? Take a vacation?"

"Oh, I can't take a vacation alone. Besides, I have to run the floral shop."

"It's been quite a year for you. You should have some time to relax."

Maddy suddenly felt the urge to ask Kate about her father.

"Kate, do you ever think about your dad?"

"Why would you ask me that?"

"Well, Cody has been asking about him. I wondered if you ever think about him?"

"No. Garrett loves me so much. It feels good to know he will never leave me. Why would I think about someone who hurt us?"

"I need to talk to you about something. I've been putting it off, but I think I need to get it off my mind."

"Okay. I'd love to talk about it with you, but I have to meet Garrett at the job site. I can call you later?"

"Kate, I'll call you. Have a good day, dear."

Maddy thought how talking to Kate in person would have been better. She was afraid of her reaction if she told her about the letter. She suddenly felt like her ex-husband was intruding in her life even though he wasn't physically here.

The boys finally went to camp. Some friends who wanted to start a yard sale invited Maddy to join in. Maddy asked Rosy for some help. It felt good to get out and become useful with so much weighing on her mind.

"Maddy, I'm having Josh bring some furniture for the sale. Did you have anything you wanted to sell?"

"No. You know me; I can't get rid of anything. Most of what is in my house was Karen's."

"Thank you for helping out."

Rosy looked at Maddy, noticing something was on her mind.

"Maddy, are you okay?"

"Oh, I'm fine. Let's get this sale started."

"Maddy, I know you too well. Did you talk to the boys again about Daryl?"

"I talked to Cody, but I didn't mention much about him. I tried to tell Kate but that failed. I got a call from my friend from New York. Daryl is trying to find me."

"What do you think he wants?"

"I'm not sure. I don't want him to find me."

"Are you afraid of him?"

"I don't know. I don't know what his motive is. It could be a number of things."

"He doesn't know where you live so that should relax you a bit."

"You would think that, but I'm not sure if he is researching me out."

Rosy gave Maddy a hug, reassuring her. There wasn't anything she could do except try to forget that he tried to find her. She took Rosy by the hand and the two women went to work to help the community sell their items. Maddy passed out some business cards and offered her services to many of the buyers in the area. She now had her smile back helping out and making new friends. Rosy was a good friend to many in the community. She always knew how to make Maddy, and her family feel better.

Maddy didn't want to pretend to be okay with Daryl. She really needed to deal with it. She sat in her house waiting for tea water to come to a boil before going into the backyard. She sat in her rattan chair and listened to the fountain trickling. She began to cry. She remembered the pain of becoming alone and having her children by her side. No money, no home, no car, struggling to stay above water. Even though that was some time ago, the memory of what she went through tortured her broken heart. Standing at the bus station after Daryl left, replayed in her mind. She entered into the unknown, not knowing where their next meal was coming from or where they would sleep. Daryl returning would bring back all that pain. And telling Kate, what would that be like? What would happen to her and Kate's relationship? All she thought about was that pain could come back into her life. Daryl Parker was not welcomed in her world any longer.

# Chapter 7

Callen went to the university. He was hoping to see Cassie roaming the halls. Being an intern suited Callen. He was easing his way into becoming a teacher, and he loved being at the school. He had permission from the Dean of the college to be an intern because of Callen's natural ability to understand difficult mathematics. He was going to be a student soon and that gave him confidence. Walking down the hall after finishing his meeting with Matt, he glimpsed Cassie talking with her friend. Callen wasn't shy, but he was a bit hesitant to show this new side of himself. He decided to approach her.

"Hi. Cassie, right?"

"Oh, I remember you. Calvin?"

"Callen. I wanted to see how you are since I bumped into you."

"I survived. Now that I got to see you again, I wanted to know if you would like to get together sometime?"

"Yes. I thought maybe we could get to know each other better, as friends of course."

"You want to get a coffee at the cafeteria? I have time before my ride gets here."

"Sure, I'd like that. You'll have to forgive me for being slow. I have this trick leg that is stubborn."

"I think you walk fine. Do you always have that cane with you?"

"I'm hoping it won't be with me much longer. I hate it, but my knee is still weak."

They took their coffee to a table near the window. Looking across from her, Callen noticed her strange look.

"What? Do I look funny, or do I have something on my face?" he asked.

"No. I was just wondering why you want to be a math teacher. It never was a subject I was good at."

"I have this gift I guess, you could say, for figuring out numbers. I've always been into math equations."

Well, architects use math. Did you ever want to be one of those?"

"No. I wanted to be a tax attorney, but it's not for me. So, what's your story, future history teacher? Why that field?"

"My dad was a history teacher. He died last year. I just wanted to carry on his legacy. I like antiques, the story of where it came from, who it belonged to. I guess that's kinda like history with a mystery."

"My mom likes antiques. I think it's cool you like vintage things."

"My dad was such a big influence on me. He loved old furniture and stuff like that. I got it from him. So, why are you using a cane? I mean, if you are private about it, you don't have to answer."

"I was in an accident a couple of years ago. I had a few surgeries to repair it."

"You're young, maybe it will get better soon."

"Do you think I look like a freak using it?"

"No. I hardly notice it. It doesn't bother me. But I know you have to be the one to live with it. It doesn't define who you are, I'm sure"

"Thank you for that."

"Oh, I gotta go. My ride will be here in five minutes."

"Cassie, would you like to meet again, just to talk. I just moved back to Santa Barbara and I'm settling in."

"I think I can do that. Will you be here tomorrow?"

"No. I don't meet with Matt until next Wednesday."

"Oh, there is this place I like to go to. It's a park that was brought to life by a local landscaper; Garrett, somebody. Do you want to meet there?"

"Garrett is my brother. He and his wife got that park in shape."

"No way! Wow, I didn't know that. I know the landscaper's brother."

"Yep, that's me."

"So, how about it?" Cassie asked.

"You're on. After class?"

"Is four o'clock okay?"

"Yeah."

"Great, see you then."

Callen was thinking, 'What just happened?' He had such a nice time with Cassie even if it was just a short time. She had a twinkle in her eye. She saw past the imperfections he focused on. He trusted her words when she said she didn't feel bothered by the cane. That may be what Callen needed to help heal the wounds that followed him.

Charles saw Callen in the driveway.

"Hello, Son. Were you at the school today?"

"Yes. I don't go back until Wednesday."

"Do you have a moment?"

"I have a few minutes."

"I just wanted you to know you can talk to me about anything. I also had a lot to think about while you were away. I wanted to make up for the times we didn't get to spend quality time together. Are there any other reasons why you came home?"

"Can I just come home? I mean, things didn't work out in Florida. What other reason is there?"

"Well, just know that I will listen if you need me."

"Dad, I'm fine. Thank you for wanting to be there."

Charles sensed Callen was hiding something. He couldn't pinpoint what it was. He wasn't going to call David to get more information. He would have to wait until he was ready to come forward. Charles was going to be prepared for anything Callen went through or had to tell him. His love would not change even if Callen never reached out to him.

Callen's meet with Cassie was soothing to him. She was already walking around the park. As they neared Kate and Garrett's tree, they both smiled. He felt like a giddy teenager with his first crush. Cassie was blond and slender, a little taller than most girls. The sun had left freckles on her cheeks and nose. She wore braces at one time as a young child. All grown up, her smile was a welcome to a tired and wounded man. They talked for hours about school, family, and the hardships of their teenage years. Cassie loved family but since her father died, she felt like the important piece of her family left her without hope of being whole. Callen shared his struggle with his leg, the accident, and connecting with his father. This meeting wasn't just building a friendship, it was emotional. While Callen spoke of his trials, Cassie touched his hand. She listened intently to every word and the sound of his voice. His heart was good. She didn't think of him as broken. He felt recovered by putting his trust in this woman. He wasn't afraid to reveal his pain to her.

"Callen, what you told me took so much courage. I admire you for sharing your story. It really moved me, touching my heart."

"I don't know what it is, but I have full trust in you."

"I'm a good listener and I think you are a genuine person. I'm very glad you knocked me down that day," she smiled.

"Thank you Cassie for being there."

That was just the beginning of many times Callen and Cassie met to talk. For the first time, Callen had something to feel good about.

Kate was wary of hospitals after her experiences visiting Karen, Callen, and Charles. Garrett and Kate chose to use a midwife for the birth of their first child. They had an appointment to see if they were finally pregnant.

"Kate, it's good to see you. Are you taking your vitamins?"

"Yes. Do you have some news for us?"

"I do. Congratulations, you are going to be parents!"

"Did you hear that?"

Kate jumped into Garrett's arms very happy her dream was coming true. Garrett had plans to help prepare them for the day their child would arrive.

"Kate, what should we do now?"

"I don't know."

"I want to celebrate with you, just you."

"Okay, but just don't give me special treatment. That will drive me crazy. I'm not that delicate," she joked.

"To me, you are delicate."

"Thanks for that but, no."

"Ok. Let's grab some blankets and some frozen cake. I know of a perfect date spot."

That evening with his truck bed swept out and stuffed with blankets, they parked facing the Pacific. They propped themselves up in the back and cuddled as three. Stars were bright and waves repeated their whispers. The Carrington's were going to be parents.

In the weeks that went by since the news of their baby, Kate felt the need to draw closer to Maddy. She would understand what it was like to be a mom. Kate had been tired and not feeling herself. She went to see her mother at the shop.

"Well, my favorite person. What are you doing here?"

"I have some news for you," she grinned.

"Kate, what do you have to tell me?"

"I'm pregnant. We wanted to wait a while until we told anyone, but you're the first."

"That's so exciting! How are you feeling?"

"I'm a little tired. I wasn't feeling well yesterday but the midwife said it's normal to feel that way."

"So, when are you due?"

"Well, I'm eight weeks, so in seven months? It seems like such a long time until our baby arrives."

"Enjoy time to yourselves. Babies can be a lot of work."

Maddy was being a mother even though Kate was grown. She loved passing on her wisdom to the daughter who became a woman right in front of her.

Kate collected baby clothes and decorated the room for the new addition. She had those bouts of fatigue and stopped working on her room to rest on the couch. Garrett came home to find his wife asleep. He wandered into the baby's room and noticed the wallpaper was still laying in rolls on the floor.

"Kate, wake up."

"What time is it?"

"After five. How long have you been sleeping?"

"I guess a few hours. I just haven't been feeling good today. I thought I would work on the room, and I got sleepy."

"Do you want to eat something?"

"No. I just want to lay here."

"I'll make something for dinner."

"Please, don't make anything that smells."

Garrett was concerned with Kate not feeling herself lately. He planned to call the midwife the next morning just to be sure.

That night, Kate woke up with abdominal cramping. She was in the bathroom crying when Garrett came in to check on her. Kate was bleeding and Garrett grabbed her coat.

"Garrett, what's happening?"

"I don't know. We'll get you in the hospital and find out."

"I don't like hospitals."

"Honey, we have no choice."

Garrett wheeled Kate into the emergency room. They admitted her and he waited to hear how the love of his life was doing. He paced thinking about the baby and Kate.

"Mr. Carrington, your wife is going to be fine. But she has had a miscarriage. She lost the baby. I'm so sorry. You can come in and see her in an hour."

Garrett felt shattered. His world was broken, and he couldn't hold Kate to get him through it. He lost his child, the child they longed and waited for. He knew it was going to be hard for Kate to accept. Going outside to get some air, he started to cry with his hands covering his face. Kate had her heart set on this being the beginning of her life as a mom. Garrett had to figure out what he was going to do to help her recover from such a big loss.

He came into her room to see her looking toward the window. She laid there feeling lost, not knowing what to think. The shock was unexpected. Garrett came by her side and put his face near her neck. He just held her. She put her hand on his head as tears rolled down her face. She made no sound as she cried. She could hear her husband crying saying, "My Kate." Their love was strong but for the first time, they wondered how they were going to get through a death of their closest family member.

After a day at the hospital, Kate was released. Being helped into the car, Kate was unsure about her future. Would she ever have a child of her own?

"Kate, we can try again."

"I can't think about that right now."

"Let's go home and you can get some rest."

Walking into their home, Garrett carried Kate into her bedroom. Her arms were wrapped around his neck. The home did not seem the same. It felt like something was missing. Garrett closed the door to the baby's room that Kate decorated. After propping some pillows behind her, Garrett brought a cup of her favorite tea to place on the nightstand. Flowers and cards arrived to lessen the pain of the sad news. When Maddy arrived, Kate knew she needed a mother's comfort.

Late in the afternoon, Kate sat in her backyard in her robe just staring at her flower garden. The red-leafed Maple appeared less bright, less significant than before. A few days went by since she lost the baby, but it felt like months. She hadn't moved from her spot when Garrett came to her. She was barefooted, propping her feet onto the chair she sat in. Her hair was tied in a ponytail. She was in deep thought, reflecting how she was going to move on from the pain she had in her heart.

"Love, what are you thinking about?"

"I was thinking about how I felt when we discovered we were having a baby. And now this feels so wrong. It feels like I will never get that back. I want to try again but I'm scared. What if it happens again? I should have taken better care of myself. What if this was my fault?"

"I understand how you feel, but this wasn't your fault. The midwife said you have a good chance it won't happen again. Sometimes it's nature's way if the baby is not healthy."

"I can't feel happy about anything anymore. I fell in love with my child; our child, and now it's over."

"We can get it back, Kate. Tomorrow I want you to be ready to take a trip with me. Can you do that? Can we mend together?"

"I'll try."

"I'm here. I loved our child too. It hurts. We will have a family, I promise."

The next day Garrett packed the car for a two-day trip. He knew Kate was feeling depressed and needed her husband to ease her pain.

"Where are you taking me? You packed a lot of things for a couple of days."

"I want you comfortable. This is for you. I want to be with you today."

As they drove, Kate fell asleep in the car. Garrett touched her hand as she laid there. He knew he needed this trip as well. The amount of grief he saw his wife going through pierced right through him and he felt the need to be strong for her. This was his special woman, the woman who changed his life and brought healing to his family. She didn't want to be delicate, but deep inside he knew she was. He would do anything for her. This trip was going to take them back to the journey when their love was new.

As Garrett stopped the car, Kate yawned and stretched.

"Where are we?"

"You're awake. Good. We are at Yosemite."

"Where?"

"This place is ours. There is so much history here. This is where I grew more in love with you."

"Garrett, I can't believe you brought me here."

"I brought a lunch for us, and we can take a slow walk and make some new memories."

Kate looked around at the trees and it revived the romantic feeling to be in the place Garrett called 'theirs.' He came to her, taking her hand and walked her over to where the shade was. She was looking at the bark and remembering how Garrett visualized the trees as he drew them. She reached out to touch the bark.

"I almost forgot what it was like to be here. Touching this tree makes me feel like I'm home."

"You are my home, Kate. I brought you here to help you reconnect with who you are inside. This is where you belong."

She embraced him, breathing in renewed life. Walking hand in hand, they hiked the same trail where their love grew. She was getting her smile back. Rounding the trail they arrived at the view of the divided mountain.

"I love looking at this mountain. It reminds me of where we were not so long ago. It's still beautiful," Kate said sincerely.

"You taught me how to love. We went through the toughest thing we could imagine, and we still have each other. Your love brought me closer, healing what was lost."

"I didn't go to that sad place alone. I had you all this time and I am grateful for what you did for me."

"It's all for you. You mean everything to me, Kate."

"Do you still want to try to have another baby?"

"Yes, but our midwife said we should give it a little more time. Right now, we need to be emotionally ready. I'll support you until it's time."

That day, Garrett gave everything to Kate. He brought the banana muffins with cream cheese frosting she kept in the freezer. His attention helped her to see how deep his love went. He knew it was going to take time for them to get over their loss.

During the weeks that passed, they focused on each other and the exterior of the home. Kate got back to her writing. She left the room she made for her baby alone. She kept the door closed to avoid seeing into it. Kate was a slow healer. She had to go through her grieving process and wait for her emotions to settle. There were good days and sad days. But no matter what kind of day she was having, Garrett was always there.

# Chapter 8

Maddy was working with a wedding planner who needed assistance in picking out floral arrangements for an event. She needed to be at the shop during that month because June weddings were popular. When the new shipment of florals arrived, her shop was filled with fragrance. The smell of Eucalyptus and Carnations wafted all around the front of the store. A few months had passed since Kate's loss. Maddy spent time comforting Kate, encouraging her to take time to write. It seemed to be a helping.

Kate submitted some manuscripts to her editor in hopes that soon she would publish her novels. Life for her was slowly getting back to normal. The tree Garrett planted for her was thriving and vibrant. It had become the focal point of their backyard.

Maddy went to check the mailbox. She noticed there was a letter from New York. It was addressed to her floral shop. It was from Daryl. She became terrified. How did he know where she worked? Why would he find her? She was alone walking to her car. Was he was somewhere watching her? Was he even in California? She waited until she was home to read the letter. She thought that she should contact him to reduce her fear of his location. She didn't really know him anymore. What kind of person was he? It was important for her to figure it out as soon as possible. She went to her home office and opened the envelope, shaking while she tore into it.

*Madeline,*

*I know you are wondering how I found where you are. I was tortured not knowing how you and the children are. Jo told me you moved to California, and I hired a private detective to find you. Please don't be afraid that I found you this way. So much has changed these past years. I need to see you. Please contact me as soon as you can. I have enclosed my phone number. I'm doing well and I have a good job. If you are wondering, yes, I am alone. I no longer have the love of my life or my child. It's hard to write these thoughts and I know what you must think of me. I have so much I need to tell you. You are the only family I have. All I want is a chance for you to just hear me. I want to see my children. You never wrote me, so I assumed you didn't want to have anything to do with me. I understand. Please call me anyway. Give me a chance to explain some things to you. Daryl*

Maddy wasn't sure what to think of his words. He sounded desperate. She had to call him and find out what he needed from her. It would ease her mind.

"Hello," he answered.

"Hello, Daryl. It's Madeline."

"I'm glad you called. How are you?"

"I have to admit, I was a little scared you wrote me. You sounded so desperate. Really though, a private detective? That made me more nervous. I don't like that you had me afraid, and I don't know what it is you want from me. I hate the way you found me. Why are you doing this now?"

"I'm sorry. I didn't mean to sound creepy. I wanted to come to California to see you. I miss our children."

"I haven't told them much about you. They know you left us. But Katharine won't take the news very well if you want to see her."

"She must hate me."

"No, she doesn't hate you. You left a daughter alone without the father she needed. I'm not sure how you are going to fix that."

"Madeline, I'm better. I got help, I have a good job, and I feel ready to see them."

"I don't know if this is a good time to see them. My mind is confused as to what to do."

"Please don't think I'm crazy. I'm still a father. I know it's been years since I've seen them, but I want a chance to prove myself, to be trusted."

"You said you are no longer with Annie and your son Connor. What happened to them?"

"It's hard to talk about."

"I need to know."

"We had a good life together. We bought a house, I was seeing my psychiatrist and keeping a job. We were all together for six years. Then one night, Annie was coming home from a friend's house on a visit. She didn't see the car coming toward her. It was a drunk driver who changed our world in one night. I lost both of them."

"Oh Daryl. I'm so sorry. My heart is breaking for you. How long ago did this happened?"

"Two years ago. I had to take a leave from work to grieve. I couldn't function or cry. Going through Annie's things, I smelled her perfume, I touched her clothes, I looked at our wedding picture and I just broke down."

"Is this why you are trying to contact me?"

"No, there are so many reasons why I need to see you. I know we will never get back to where we used to be. I'm alone Madeline, very alone. I sold my house to get into something smaller. I saved up enough money to make the trip. Will you let me come see you?"

"Daryl, I have to think about it. I know this is a rough time for you. I don't want to shock the kids. Let me tell them first."

"Jo said Karen died. She was a wonderful woman. I'm sorry for your loss as well."

"Thank you for that. It still hurts that she's gone."

"I'm glad you called me. I will give you some time to talk to the children."

"I don't know how I'm going to tell Katharine."

"When you do talk to them, please tell them their father loves them."

"I will. I'll call you soon. Goodbye Daryl."

"Bye, Madeline."

After Maddy hung up the phone, she laid on her bed exhausted. All the pain and memory of Daryl leaving resurfaced again. She was afraid to have him see the children. It was a tough decision for her. This was going to change her life. He obviously wanted to be part of her family again. How was she going to explain to Chase and Cody who this man was? Maddy put the letter away with the others. She took out a picture of Daryl standing with her and the kids years ago. That photo was the happiest she and Daryl ever were. After that, it all became evident things were ending for this family. Once again, Maddy was going to have to use the strength she built up to face another challenge. She would have to try to relax her mind for the evening. Sleep was what she needed to think this through.

A few weeks went by since Maddy and Daryl talked. She hadn't called him again. She was still thinking about how and what she was going to tell them. Kate wanted to drop by Maddy's house to retrieve a scarf she left when she moved out. While organizing her own closet, she noticed the hand-knitted scarf from Karen was missing.

"I hope this isn't a bad time. I'm doing some sorting and my favorite scarf was missing."

"I didn't see it around. You can look around and try to find it. Maybe it's still in your old room."

"What are you doing today? You look a little distressed, Mom."

"I have a lot on my mind. I have orders to fill and vendors to call so it's a busy life for someone in the flower business."

"I can see that."

Kate loved going upstairs in this house. The beauty and the style of it brought back many memories of her aunt Karen. Going into the room, she began searching the closet. Moving some old boxes to find the scarf, under one box were envelopes from Daryl. Kate shut the door and proceeded to look through them. She caught her breath while reading.

"What?" she thought aloud.

She had so many things running through her mind. Why would her mother keep this from her? Reading that he wanted to come to California had Kate upset, afraid of what would change for her and her brothers. She was angry, betrayed, and saddened. She had to confront her mother about this. Kate gathered up the letters and ran down stairs to the kitchen where Maddy was.

"Mom, I think you have something to tell me."

"What? What do I have to tell you?"

"Really, you don't think you should have told me about these."

Kate slammed the envelopes on the kitchen island.

"Oh no, Kate!"

"You sure didn't hide these very well. Although if you did, I wouldn't have found them. Explain yourself! Why did he write you!?"

"You listen to me young lady, I don't have to explain anything to you! I was going to work it out with him before I gave him an answer."

"You were actually going to have him come here! How could you do that to us?"

"I wasn't making any decisions until I talked to you three. I was thinking it through."

"You lied to me. We have been okay without him for nine years and now he wants to be back in our life?"

"I think we should hear his side of things," Maddy explained.

"You should have talked to me about this when you got the letter. I don't want to see him. If you decide to let him come here, I won't see him!"

"That is up to you. You are a grown woman, but the boys are still young, and they have been asking about their father. I owe them that even if you don't agree with it."

"I need to get out of here. You really disappointed me, Mom. How could you take him back?"

"Kate, I didn't take him back. Believe me, I wanted to tell you."

"But I found out this way instead."

"Kate, don't leave angry with me. I was doing the best I could about this. Please understand that."

Kate left. The news was too much for her emotions to take. Maybe she should see her father and give him a piece of her mind. She wanted to hurt him with her words and let him feel the pain her family went through. She wasn't thinking clearly at the moment. She worried for her brothers. Kate didn't know what her mother would decide. Whatever it was, Kate would not be any part of it, no matter the cost.

Maddy held the envelopes in her hand as she walked up the stairs to put them away. She didn't want to lose Kate's trust, especially that way. She couldn't wait any longer to tell Daryl. The boys needed to talk with their mother about the father that left them.

It was a Saturday and Maddy wanted to sit with her boys and let them in on the secret. She had to take them away from their playtime outside. This was going to be hard for her to find the words to ease them into the history of the man they wanted to know.

"Come sit on the couch, boys."

"Are we in trouble?" Chase asked.

"No, honey. No one's in trouble. I just wanted to talk to you about your father."

"We don't remember him, but we want to know about him," said Cody.

"Well, he wrote me a letter and he wants to come see you. Just a visit, he's not going to take you away."

"When is he coming?" Chase asked.

"I don't know. I haven't talked to him about that. When do you think he should come?"

"How about right now?" said Chase.

"No, not right now. He's in New York so he would have to plan the trip. What do you think Cody, do you want to see him?"

"Why does he want to see us now? What if he moves here? I don't know him."

"I know, honey. He is your dad and he's been through a lot. He used to be married after we divorced, and his wife is not with him anymore."

"What happened to her, Mom?"

"She died. So, maybe we can make him feel welcomed if we decide to let him come visit."

"What about Kate? Can she see him too?"

"Kate doesn't want to see her dad right now. We can give her some time to think it over."

"Is he a good person, Mom?" asked Chase.

"I think he might be. We'll give him a chance. That would be the kind thing to do, not judge him so harshly."

Chase was feeling grown up even if he was only twelve.

"Mom, I think you should do what you think is best. I don't know what I would say to him. It's weird, you know," Cody reflected.

"Just ask him questions, feel free to be yourselves. I'll be right there with you when you see him. Would that be okay?"

"I think it will be okay, Mom," Chase said.

"Will he stay here?" Cody asked.

"No. He will stay in a hotel."

"If he's our Dad, why can't he stay here?" Chase asked.

"Well, he's a stranger in a sense so, I think it would be appropriate for him to stay in a hotel."

Maddy wrapped her arms around her boys, feeling glad that it went so well. Maddy called Daryl and confirmed he could make the trip soon and stay for three days. He asked if he could call Kate and talk to her, but Maddy let him know she was not ready to take that step.

Kate was home writing when Garrett returned from working on a new nursery outside of town. He had an hour before he needed to leave again. She told him about her dad's letters and how her mother wanted to visit them.

"I was so angry with her. I can't believe she wants to meet with him."

"Maybe you should see it from her perspective."

"Whose side are you on?"

"It's not about taking sides, it's about what the boys need. Maybe Daryl is different and it's time the boys got to know him."

"You have no idea what it was like for me. I was old enough to know him. We were a family and it all got destroyed by him. I don't think I can forgive him for that."

"I can understand how you feel. What if you gave him a chance to explain himself and then decide?"

"I don't think I can."

"I know you'll do the right thing. And Kate, that is your mother. You may not have a lot of things, but you will always have her as your mother. Think about it."

Garrett went outside to check how the Oranges were ripening. Kate sat at her table thinking about what he said. She then came outside to talk to Garrett.

"I love you Garrett. I'm sorry if I sounded upset."

"I know. It's okay if you are upset. A lot has happened to your family. I think you need to talk to your mom about how you feel. Put yourself in her place."

She wrapped her arms around his waist and kissed him for his honest words. She knew he was right, and she needed to find the right words to say to Maddy.

"Love, I'm going to go see Callen now. I'll be back in two hours. I have some chili slow-cooking on the stove for tonight's dinner. I thought I'd give you a hand today," Garrett said.

"Thank you! It does smell good. I'll see you soon."

"Love you," Garrett called back.

Garrett wanted to visit with Callen about his thoughts on getting back into physical therapy. Callen had talked about wanting to stop using the cane and get his knee back in good working shape.

"Hey, how's it going, Brother?"

"Good. I tried to help Mom in the garden and got a little sore sitting on the ground. It's so hard not being able to bend my knee without it aching."

"That's what I wanted to talk to you about. I got the number of a good physical therapist who specializes in sports injuries like your knee."

"You know, I have been to so many good ones. I've had three surgeries. What makes you think this time it will work differently?"

"Well, I don't know, but we can keep trying. Have you had an MRI?"

"It's been over a year ago."

"I know you're discouraged. I also know you want to ditch the cane, right?"

"Yeah, I do."

"Call them. Try to get an appointment."

"Do you always have to be so bossy?" Callen joked.

"I am the older brother. So, what else has been going on lately? Dad said you've been at the university."

"I have been following my mentor until I can enroll."

"You still want to be a teacher?"

"Yeah, I think it's a good decision."

"What happened to your plan to be an attorney?"

"It was just a reminder of who I used to be. I felt this career change was a perfect for me."

"I'm still proud of you. I hope you know that."

"I do. I didn't tell you, but I met someone at the school. Cassie, she's a history student."

"That's great. How do you feel about being in a relationship?"

"I still feel like I have to learn all over again how to have a girlfriend. Also, David's upset with me because I won't go to his wedding."

"Did you have anxiety while in Florida?? Is that why you can't go?

"Yes. I have occasional moments of panic, but I think I need to see someone about it."

"You're headed in the right direction. It will all come together."

"I can't wait to burn this cane."

"We'll burn it together."

The brothers were in a good place in their lives. Garrett could only imagine what was going on in Callen's head. The stress of the accident wasn't behind him yet. Callen didn't want Kate to know about the wreck he was going through. He had trust in Garrett implicitly. As a brother, all Garrett could do was try to help Callen get the right help toward normal. He was alive, he was still a member of his family. Now an invader was present, and this was not going to be easy for Callen to work on. Anxiety and seeing a physical therapist were things Callen would have to accept in order to get well and regain his control. Garrett was caring and willing to do whatever it took to help Callen reach the goal of emotional health. Callen kept the degree of anxiety to himself. He shared that he needed help, but Garrett was in for a surprise. Just how bad was Callen's condition? Garrett would soon find out how much love was required to conquer a wounded heart.

# Chapter 9

Charles didn't know much about why Callen was doing an internship at the university. The two had not had a full conversation since Callen came back. Charles thought he would ask Mary if she knew anything.

"Mary, is Callen home?"

"No, Dear. He went to the university again."

"Do you know why he is going there? I know he's not enrolled in school. He said he is an intern. Do you know anything else about it?"

"No. I don't know why you two haven't talked."

"He's so hard to reach. He doesn't want to share what he wants to do in his life for some reason."

"He is a grown man. Aren't you happy he's here and not in Florida?"

"Of course I am. I think he's afraid to talk to me. I haven't agreed with some of the choices he made, and it has caused friction between us."

"Well, maybe you should try to talk to him again. He usually gets back after four. Take the time to try to support and help him."

"Of course."

Charles took a deep breath and walked to his office. He had to think of what he could say without escalating tension. Charles was feeling a bit guilty for not having been there when he should have. Was Callen holding on to some resentment or fear that his father created? He felt like a cannon ready to go off when he thought of their last argument.

Callen was at the school early just to see if he could see Cassie again. He was on his way to the cafeteria to meet Matt when he saw Cassie in the library. He could see her through the hall window. It made him smile. Walking in, he felt nervous. He thought about her every day and wanted to get to know her better. He liked her smile, her hair, and her special way of giving him attention when he talked to her.

"Hello, Cassie."

"Callen. Are you doing some work in here too?"

"No. I saw you in the window as I passed by."

She adjusted her seat, "I come here early to catch up on my studies."

"I'm not sure if you have time, but I would like to see you again. I don't have too many friends here since I moved back, but I like talking to you."

"I would really like that," Cassie said.

Callen watch Cassie write something.

"Here's my home phone number. Call me when you would like to do something."

"Ok. I'll do that."

Callen was walking toward the door when Cassie called out almost too loudly, "Callen, just to let you know, I'm into pink Roses. They are my favorite," she smiled.

"I'll remember that." Her smile was enough to light up Callen's heart.

He was looking for a friend in Cassie. For now, he was going to ignore his trauma. He hadn't experienced issues with anxiety or people in public. Since his diagnosis, he had been extra cautious. With Cassie, he didn't feel that way. He had never developed a friendship so trusting since Kate.

Coming home, Callen found Charles in the backyard. He was waiting for his son to get home.

"Hey, Dad. Are you coming in for dinner?"

"Not right now. I wanted to talk to you. You know, catch up."

"Okay, what's on your mind?"

"What are you doing at the university? Your mom says you're an intern."

"Does this disappoint you?"

"Why would it disappoint me?"

"Because I'm not making money. I decided to change my career."

"Oh. What are you wanting to do?"

"Don't laugh. I want to be a math teacher. I think I can be very good at it."

"Why did you change your mind about being an attorney?"

"Does it matter? What's important is that I'm doing something I love."

"Well then, I guess it doesn't matter to me if that is your choice."

"Now you're sounding like I'm not thinking straight about my ambitions."

"You will have to go to school for a lot of years and teachers don't make that much money."

"Do you really think money is what is going to make me a better man?"

"I just don't want you to struggle. Life is hard."

"You don't have to tell me about how hard life is. No one knows that better than me. I knew that this wasn't going to go anywhere. We just can't agree."

"What am I supposed to think, Callen? You came home after not speaking to us for months, then you decide to be an intern and you have no job prospects."

"You have no idea what I went through to get my life back. Out of all people, I thought you would be the one to understand that."

"I can guess how hard it was for you. To me, it feels as though you are hiding something. There is another reason you came home. Do you want to tell me? Are you in debt? Do you need money?"

"I'm done with this conversation. You make it very hard to live here with you when you grill me with doubt and questions about why I'm here. I'm your son and it shouldn't matter."

"I guess you're right. I hope the choice you make will help you out and you get exactly what you want." Charles had sarcasm in his voice.

"And if I fail, are you going to say, 'I told you so?'"

"I won't say that, but I hope you prove me wrong."

"How can you kick me when I'm down?"

"Are you down? I just want you to learn from my mistakes."

"Dad, I never learned anything from you. I crawled out of the pit without you. When are you going to get it? I'm better off without you."

Callen stumbled as he hurriedly stood up. He walked off before his father could see his tears. It seemed that each time he felt low, he couldn't give up without a fight. He felt beaten by Charles. He was going to have to prove his father wrong. Pulling himself up was hard but not hard enough to give up.

Callen called Garrett to see if he could stay with him for a few days. The tension was too much for Callen. Living under the same roof as his father was breaking down his will to try things on his own. How could Charles hold disbelief in Callen? He thought things were good between him and his father. Not perfect, but good enough. Charles always had high expectations for his children. He thought if they listened to him, they would fair less badly in life.

Callen was a grown man who felt able to take care of himself. It hurt him to think his father still didn't believe in him. He wasn't sure what was going to convince his father.

"Callen, what's going on?"

"Hey, Brother. Do you mind if I stay at your place for a few days? Dad just laid into me with his so-called words of advice. I need a break from him."

"Did you tell him about your anxiety?"

"No. Why should I? He'll just judge me like he always does."

"Okay, you can stay here for two days. I'll let Kate know. You are eventually going to have to reveal what you are experiencing."

"I don't know. It doesn't matter what I say, he'll just give his opinion and make me feel low."

"I found an orthopedic doctor who wants to look at your knee and leg."

"Thanks. And thanks for not judging me, Garrett."

Callen went to his room to pack a bag. His mother overheard his conversation with Garrett.

"Callen, I heard you on the phone."

"I'm sorry, Mom. I can't get through to him. He doesn't think I'm capable of being the man I want to be."

"I understand. Don't let things go unsaid for too long. I don't know why he feels that way. He just wants  you to be happy."

"I wish I believed that."

His mother drove him to Garrett's home. Mary was feeling upset at Charles even though she tried to be a supportive wife. She had enough of the distance between father and son who needed love. Her face showed pain when she returned home.

"Charles, what did you say to Callen?"

"What difference does it make? He's set on doing things his own way."

"He is our son. He is a grown man. Aren't you proud of him for his effort?"

"So, now I don't know what's best for my son? I guess I can no longer give him my advice."

"Stop sounding pathetic! He loves you. You refuse to see what he's struggling with. Can't you see it?"

"That's just it, he won't tell me what he's going through. Something happened in Florida, I know it."

"Charles, put that behind you. He's here, safe, and he needs you."

"He should tell me that. I can't read his mind."

"He shouldn't have to. You can serve yourself dinner. I'm going to my room."

Charles could do nothing but hang his head. He never expected Mary to feel that way. As she shut the door, she began to sob. Her words were strong, but she was displaying boldness for the sake of her son. She did love her husband, but she loved Callen just as much. This was a woman who could have been looking at pictures of her son who experienced death. Each day she prayed for his safety and his well-being. She didn't want Callen to leave, even if was going to Garrett's. She wanted the wounds to heal in her family. In time, Mary would know the reason Charles wanted to find real answers about Callen's return.

"I hope you like this bed. Garrett got it after we lost our baby." Kate's warm voice reached him. "I think it's nice to have a guest stay with us."

"I was very sorry about your loss. I know you would have made a great mother."

"We're not ready to try again. I'm still not right with it."

"It will get better. So, aren't you going to ask me why I'm here?"

"You can tell me when you are ready. I don't need to ask."

"It's my dad. He just won't be proud of how far I've come. It's as if he's waiting for me to fail."

"Garrett says you intern at the university. Do you like the atmosphere, I mean college life?"

"I do. I met someone there. Actually I knocked her down not looking where I was going."

"Oh wow! Who is she? Is she a student?"

"Yes. Her name is Cassie Adams. She wants to be a History teacher."

"Have you been dating?"

"Once. Not really a date. I want to see her again. She told me what her favorite flowers are. Roses, pink Roses."

"I think that means she likes you."

"I hope so. I want to give it a chance."

Kate was happy for Callen. She smiled as she left the room. "Wash up. Dinner is almost ready."

"Thanks, Kate."

"Sure. Callen, everything will work out with you and your dad."

Kate loved seeing the three of them sitting together talking and having a meal. It was a sense of calm and peaceful enjoyment for the family. Callen needed to be around a positive environment. Kate always had a way of helping him feel good about himself. Soon enough with hope, he would get what he longed for since childhood, his father's love and approval.

After the fire went out in the fireplace and the house cooled off, everyone retired to bed. Callen had been replaying his disagreement with Charles, and it made him anxious. Turning off the light, Callen laid in his bed hoping to fall asleep quickly without thinking for the night, but he tossed all night. He was having a dream, a nightmare. He could vividly see the images in his dream. He heard his father shouting, "Don't go!" He could feel the engine rev up and the screeching of tires on the pavement. Faster and faster he sped up hugging every corner. The world became a blur. He felt like he was in a tunnel, and it was dark, too dark to see any light. In a second everything changed. Bright sparkling lights came from everywhere. Metal was scraping on the road. He could feel his leg smashing against a guard rail. He could feel his skin burning and blood running down his face. His body jumped in bed. He tried to yell for help, but no words came out. No one came to his rescue. He could hear voices from somewhere. Where were they coming from? Distorted people approached; they were blurry. He was confused as to who they were and what they wanted with him. He didn't know what happened or where he was. He tried to scream again; he tried to move. He seen death coming, he felt paralyzed. As someone tried to move him, he shouted out, "NO!" He suddenly was halfway out of his dream. Was it real? Why were they touching him? It began to feel like another night terror.

"Help me, please don't touch me!" Callen shouted.

"Garrett, did you hear that?" Kate whispered.

"Yes. Come on. Sounds like Callen."

"Help me, help me!"

Kate came to Callen's side.

"I'm here. Callen, it's Kate."

"Hold me, hold me. Help me."

Kate looked at Garrett as she tried to calm him down.

"What's happening? Garrett, why is he like this?"

"We can talk about it later. We need to take care of him right now."

Kate held Callen until he fell asleep. She rocked him like a child as his breathing slowed down. She streamed tears as he cried from the trauma he had been through. As he drifted back to sleep, Garrett took Kate into the kitchen to fill her in on what Callen was experiencing.

"Garrett, what is going on?"

"Callen was diagnosed with PTSD, a disorder caused by trauma. The accident left more than scars. It causes him to have bouts of anxiety and fear."

"Garrett, what is he going to do?"

"He has to get help. This is why he can't talk to Dad."

"I think Charles should know. Does Mary know?"

"I don't think so. Callen is different. He wants things to be different."

"Do you think your father will be understanding to what he's feeling?"

"I don't know. Dad may not believe in therapy or that he even needs help."

"We have to do something."

"Callen has to make that decision. I might have to step in and help though."

"I never imagined he was going through this. I want to do something to make it better."

"You can't, Kate. I'll talk to Callen about it another time. Let's give him these few days to think on it."

Kate felt lost. She knew Callen had changed but observing his nightmare left her feeling like she needed to come to his rescue. Charles would need to let go of what it was that was keeping him from believing in his son. He was the type of man who held in his feelings. It was hard to express himself. Garrett wasn't going to tell him about Callen's pain. However he was going to let him know how he felt about his brother and help him get the love he deserved. Callen needed his father's love.

# Chapter 10

Maddy planned to visit with Kate to better explain about her father and his letters. The boys were at their friends' home spending the night and Maddy was home alone.

She recalled the day she met Daryl. She was still seventeen and he was a year older. Madeline was a typical teenager. She loved the latest style clothes, makeup, and being with her friends. She didn't have a boyfriend yet. Most of the boys she knew were immature and were after more than a sweet romance. She loved being herself, a happy teenager who never knew her father. She had so many women in her life to guide her; two grandmothers and mother. Her sister Karen, was more interested in her career and success and was in no hurry to find love or marry. Madeline was different. She wanted to explore what was out there for her. Her friends planned to stick by her forever. She had it all until she saw Daryl Parker. He was ruggedly handsome, fit, and clean. His auburn wavy hair was a little longer than most. His teeth were straight, and his voice was rich and deep. His skin was tanned, probably from working in the fields picking vegetables for a local grower. He was an only child. He was good at hiding who he was. He had good looks, but he was lonely. He missed his parents who were killed in a car accident when he was ten. At eighteen, the years seemed like yesterday when he lost them. He never stopped loving them. He made a few friends, but he carried his sadness with him. He was placed in foster care temporarily until permanently placed with his grandmother. He kept to himself during his early teenage years. He managed to stay in school and keep out of trouble. At first, he spent time searching photos of his beloved family wondering why this happened to them. At one point, it became too painful to keep looking at them.

Madeline was a bright student, she loved completing her homework assignments and kept perfect attendance. She noticed Daryl when he came out of the school office. When they had noticed each other, their eyes met with a flirtatious look. She was flattered by his beautiful smile. She noticed his toned arms and the way his clothes fit his body. He was nice to look at. She turned around and he ran after her.

"I've seen you around. You're in my math class. I sit in the back."

"Yeah, I know. I'm Madeline."

"Daryl. I've always wanted to talk to you, but I don't know how to open conversations very well."

"I think you're doing quite well."

"Really? I thought I sounded nervous."

"You do, but I think you are better than you know."

"Well, I'll see you around. It was nice to meet you."

"Wait a minute. You want to hang out sometime? It's just nice to talk to someone new," she ventured.

Daryl grinned again, "I would like that."

Days went by and Maddy and Daryl became a couple. There had good times and good talks. His tender kiss and muscular arms were just what she needed to feel that she could spend the rest of her life with him. He would hold her and exude comfort. She listened and gave him attention, something he truly needed. He was in love and so was she. Two young hearts embracing new love and making plans to stay together. After school was over, Daryl and Madeline were married. Everything was good until life presented its usual difficulties. Daryl became distant and angry. He couldn't find a good enough job to pay for the lifestyle he thought Madeline wanted. They struggled, sometimes not having enough to eat. Madeline hesitantly asked to borrow money from Karen to keep the lights and water on. There were times Daryl felt that his love for Madeline was more than enough. He wanted to be a good husband and father. Then there were times when he had that haunting feeling when he thought of every struggle he was going through. The negative emotions took its toll and he needed release. He had to abandon his family for their sake and his.

Madeline was left exposed in a place where she never had been. Family had always meant love and security. Now she was devastated that the man she loved disappeared. She knew she needed strength to care for what was left of her family. It was time to rebuild for the sake of her children.

Maddy couldn't believe it had been over nine years since Daryl left. It was odd to think he again wanted to be part of their life. If she thought she was no longer hurt, she'd be lying to herself. Envisioning him returning brought it back. Kate still was not speaking to her mother. She believed that her mother shouldn't have kept those letters from her.

Maddy was a wise and smart woman. Kate was still young and had few experiences like her mother had. Maddy felt that she did the right thing, and she wanted her daughter to understand why. Maddy still had her marriage license in a box with her divorce decree. It was a shame she was divorced. She didn't like that word. When she looked at Karen's life, she admired her good and fulfilling marriage with Michael. It was hard not to compare her bad choices in her life and marriage to Karen's. She knew that was the pain talking. As she started to fall asleep, she thought about the day Kate angrily walked out. Her father brought up some very bad memories causing fear. She didn't want that to ruin what they had built together. She would help her daughter see another perspective.

Maddy had someone come out to look at her fence in the front yard. It was rusting and needed repair. The floral trellis also needed to be replaced. As much as Maddy hated to change it, she had no choice. She wanted to keep Karen's house in good standing and continue to be her forever home. That was where she wanted to grow old, where she wanted to have her grandchildren visit. Karen would have wanted her to make new memories there. Having Daryl return was not the new memory she wanted to add.

Maddy drove to Kate's to help her understand where she was coming from. It was important to her if she was going to have Daryl be part of her children's lives. Maddy walked between the flower beds leading to Kate's porch. She could see the hard work of a landscaper and his wife. Tools and trees surrounded their property. Garrett's truck was still filled with soil, dead leaves, and branches. The front of their house was full of mixed aromas. Her daughter found what she wanted, all the flowers and trees she dreamed of having. Garrett opened the door before she could knock.

"Maddy, what a nice surprise. Come in."

"Thank you. Your place looks better every time I visit."

"Thanks. Where are the boys? Are you by yourself?

"Yes, just me. Is Kate here?"

"She's out in the back garden. Just go right around there."

"Kate."

"Mom, what are you doing here? Kind of far out for you to travel."

"It's not that far. I had to see you."

Kate was on her knees weeding out her vegetable garden and picking deadheads off the flowers. She stayed on her knees.

"About what? That you kept a secret from me?"

"Kate, what I do with your father is not your concern. I know this hurt you, but I wasn't keeping it a secret. I had to think it through and do what was best for the boys."

"You mean do what was best for you."

"Now, that's not fair. I know you're a grown woman but don't take that tone with me."

"I'm sorry. How am I supposed to feel or think about what you did?"

"What did I do? I did what any responsible parent or woman would do when her ex comes back. I have a brain, Kate. I know how to be sensible. Let me get one thing clear. I will not take your father back, no matter what he thinks. You got that?"

Kate stood up. Her knees were dirty. "I got it. I don't know what to feel if I see him."

"You need to learn to forgive, move on. You have a loving husband who will stay by you. Give Daryl a small chance, even if it's just to have closure."

"Okay, I have to think about it like you did. I can see what you were going through."

"That's all I was doing, Kate. I will do anything to protect you and the boys. Your father wanting to see me is just that, a meeting."

"What if he wants to have some kind of custody?"

"You let me worry about that. I know what is best for the boys. You know me. You can trust I will find a way to take care of it."

"Yes. I know you. I think I was just shocked that he would return," Kate admitted.

"Believe me, I am too. I can understand why you were angry. I didn't have a father. I was too young to know what it felt like to have one. But if I could, I'd love to meet him even if he did the wrong thing. I really miss a hug from you." Maddy reached out.

"I'm sorry I misjudged you, Mom."

"It's alright now, honey. I can see how all this made you feel. By the way, I noticed some bags by the door. Do you have a guest?"

"Callen needed to stay with us for a couple of days."

"Any reason why?"

"He's trying to reach out to his father who can be difficult to understand. It's funny, you have no father, I don't want to see mine, and Callen just wants his father to love him."

"Parents are an important part of a young person's life."

Kate was dirty from planting and weeding but she didn't care. She couldn't help but embrace her mother, having hopes to be a mother herself one day. Kate needed her mother's pillar of support during rough times. Maturity always took its time and Kate would be willing to forgive even if it only meant having closure with her father. She would say what she had to and be done with it. Kate wanted to protect her feelings but knew every adult deserved respect. Maddy's words sunk in deep. Kate would follow the steps her mother asked her to take if Daryl wanted to see her.

Garrett was happy to see them talking again. Standing there with his arms crossed and leaning against the door jamb, he smiled watching them hold each other.

Callen went home later in the day. Like an older brother, Garrett reminded him to see the therapist to control his night terrors. Callen was even more aware of the need to inform his father about his condition. This would be a core conversation that could tighten the two of them.

Charles had to know the whole story. Callen remembered his brother's words, that they had to love their father even if they didn't agree with him. That meant listening more. He could do it. He had to do it. Callen would need to be brave and patient. Kate's caring nature helped him to see the serious nature of this talk if he wanted to be a son. Kate was more than just a friend to Callen; she was as much his family and who could want more than that?

# Chapter 11

Garrett had called his family physician to get a referral for a good therapist to help Callen. He would have done it for anyone he cared about. But seeing his brother go through night terrors spurred him on to search for a specialist. His doctor gave him the phone number of Trevor Madison. He made the appointment for Callen.

Garrett was a mild tempered man. He would never disrespect his father. His brother and father developed an awkward relationship. He felt it was going on too long and was affecting Callen's health. Garrett had to see Charles.

"Dad, are you busy?"

"Garrett. What are you doing here? Is Kate with you?"

"No, she's not. Do you have some time? I have a problem. I need to talk about Callen."

"Callen? What about? I tell you, that boy, all he wants to do is have his way."

"We are all like that sometimes."

"Don't tell me you want to tell me what to think too. I really don't have time for all this nonsense, Garrett."

"Dad, wait. Please sit down. There is something I have to say to you."

"Alright, Son. What is it you want?"

"What is this thing between you and Callen? What is it that is keeping you from hearing him out?"

"What do you want me to say? He has his own ways. He doesn't listen to me. Do you want me to take the blame for what he is going through?"

"No. I want you to know something. You have no idea what he is going through. It's serious."

"He made some dumb choices as a kid and now he wants to be a teacher. I think he's hiding something."

"You don't know him anymore, Dad. You don't. Since his accident, he has had some difficulty sleeping, he gets anxious. In Florida he was diagnosed with PTSD."

"What is that? Isn't that from the war?"

"It means Post-Traumatic Stress Disorder. He has it bad. He spent the night at my house, and he had a night terror. It was so hard to watch him go through that. I think he goes through it quite a bit."

"Why doesn't he tell me this himself?"

"I don't think he can. He's afraid of so many things now and one of them is you."

"Me? Why would he think that? I love my son."

"I know you do. But you need to reach deeper and see who he really is. Even though he is suffering he's changed for the better. David asked him to move back here to get the help he needs. He requires care so he can get back to himself."

"I've bailed him out of so many situations I just don't know what to do for him anymore. He still owes me from when he bought his bike."

"How could you say that? If you hold his past over his head he will never get better. Just love him. Be a big support to him."

"I'm afraid he's going to screw up his life again. You don't know what it did to me when I thought I was going to lose him."

"Did you say screw up his life? Do you hear yourself? We all went through it. This isn't just about you. I'm going to be a father someday. No matter what my kids go through, I'm in their corner. If they fail, I will be there to pick them up. They will need me to be their role model to help them grow up. But if this is the way you think, nothing good is going to come to you."

"I did damage, Garrett. Maybe it's too late."

"Dad, it's not. Callen needs to see a therapist. He was seeing one in Florida, but he stopped going. He wants help again."

"Isn't that a psychiatrist?"

"No. it's just someone who specializes in this disorder. They are going to help him. Don't you want that?"

Charles felt like his world crushed him. He didn't feel like a good role model for Callen or anyone. Charles didn't put much trust in therapy. He was going to have to listen to Garrett and go with it.

"I do want him to get better. Why couldn't I see it?"

"You refused to see it. It is so easy to see our mistakes. Be proud he's going to school. He received a grant to pay for college so don't ask him about money."

"What about his leg? It looks like he is stuck using that cane."

"I don't think he is stuck forever. He is getting help with that too."

"'I misjudged him...like my father did to me. When I married your mother we had nothing. Life was very hard, then you were born. I had to work two jobs just to pay rent. I didn't want that for you or Callen."

"We all turned out fine, Dad. Ignoring this problem won't help anyone. Callen is sinking deeper into a hole of despair."

"Well, I know he won't come to me anytime soon."

"He will. In the meantime, let him know you care, somehow, If you don't, you are going to lose him."

"Does he know you're here?"

"No. I'm taking a big risk by being here. He tried to talk to you, and it backfired. I needed to step in to help a brother I lost for many years. I thought he and I would never be close again."

"You're right. I had no idea he was going through trauma. I just can't imagine him in so much pain."

"Now you know. Try to see things his way, believe that he knows what's best for him."

He looked at his son with new respect, "Alright, Garrett."

"I'm sure in time, he will pay back old debts he owes and apologize for mistakes. Like you used to tell me, "One thing at a time," for Callen's sake."

Charles tried to hide it, but he had tears building as Garrett spoke about serious issues. He knew about the distance between Callen and Garrett, and he was happy to see they worked it out. Garrett came to his aging father and put his hand on his shoulder, patting him to let him know he was understanding and respectful.

"Thank you, Son."

"I love you, Dad. I gotta go be with Kate. I stopped by here on my way home."

"You're a good man, Garrett."

"So are you."

Garrett felt the emotion inside him. He was afraid his father would not understand. Things needed to change for his family. He couldn't imagine ignoring the needs of his family if he became a father. He wanted Charles to repair the only family he had. Garrett learned many things from him. He observed the distant way Charles treated them. He learned what to do and what not to do.

There on the dashboard of his car was his reminder, a curled picture of Kate, his Kate. A breeze was gently moving her hair to the side. Her smile still mesmerized him. Garrett knew what he was living for at that moment. Kate wasn't famous or glamorous. She didn't come from the best life. But she knew how to love Garrett and he knew how to love her. She had become a landscaper's wife, and they were both proud of that. Seeing what Callen was going through, he wanted him to have what they had, a partner who would complete his life. Garrett thought to ask his wife about getting together with them and get to know her better. Garrett was not going to stop loving and encouraging Callen even if Charles was slow at it. Garrett wasn't going to lose him again.

When Garrett opened the door, he could smell it. Kate was making a pie for dessert. Garrett's favorite was cherry, and he could almost taste it as he walked into the house.

"Did you bake my favorite?"

"I did. It has to cool so, be patient. Where have you been? I thought you were going to be home early."

"Oh, I went to see Dad."

"Did you talk to him about Callen? I still can't get over that night he suffered."

"I told him about it."

"Garrett, I thought you weren't going to tell him."

"I had to. Callen won't do it."

"Are you going to tell him that you talked to Charles?"

"I am. I was thinking about you on my way home."

"Were you?"

"Yes. I appreciate you so much. My father may have difficulties showing emotion, but I don't. I love you, Kate."

He came closer. He could see her hair hanging over her eye. He took the hair away to stroke her cheek and look deeper into her eyes. He held her face in his hands for a moment and then gently kissed her lips. He kissed her long, tender, and with so much passion. Garrett gave everything to Kate. She was in love too. Wrapping her arms around his body, she could feel how much he cared for her. Kate got what she wished for; a loving man who made sure she knew she was well loved.

"I was thinking, why don't we ask Cassie and Callen to come here for dinner? I think it could be fun."

"I'd like to meet her. Do you think he would like to bring her?"

"I'll ask him."

"One more kiss before you go call him." He smiled at her and walked away.

Callen wasn't home when he called. His mother said he was out with Cassie. She would have him call when he returned.

Meanwhile, Callen was enjoying his evening with her.

"Did you say you used to ride horses?" Callen asked.

"I did more than ride them, I competed in state competitions. My father put me in equestrian lessons when I was four. I stopped riding during high school."

"Can you tell me more about your father?"

"Sure. I like talking about him. What do you want to know?"

"What did he die of?"

"Cancer. He went a long time before it got bad, about six years. We're not sure how he got it, but it took a toll on his body."

"What did you love about him?"

"Everything I can think of. He was my hero. I knew my dad wanted our relationship to be special. I was his girl."

"What about your brother?"

"He was much older than me, fifteen years older. Being the baby and the only girl, it made Dad happy. Caden, my brother, never felt left out. He moved to Vermont after high school. He comes to visit every two or three years. I miss him."

"I wish I could get close with my dad," Callen lamented.

"Why can't you?"

"He's always been the type to just ignore issues. I just connected with my brother Garrett a couple of years ago and my dad won't give me a chance to prove I can make my own decisions. He would rather tell me what I'm doing wrong."

"Sometimes when we get older, we get better. I think your dad will see it clearly."

"How did you get to be so positive, Cassie?"

"It's you that makes me feel that way."

"I think you are just trying to give me confidence."

"Callen, you already have enough for both of us."

"I think it's you who's giving it to me. You are definitely my comfort these days." He turned quickly, "Did I just say that?"

"You did."

She took the initiative to lean forward. She put her hand on his shoulder and kissed his cheek and then his lips. Callen was falling, falling deeply into someone who came to heal his heart. Her lips moved around to his ear, and she kissed his neck.

She whispered, "Callen Carrington, I've fallen in love with you. I have found what makes me happy."

He pulled back a little, "Cassie, I thought I was in love so many times. But now you know what this means? I can never let you out of my life. Cassie Adams, I love you too."

They kissed and held on to each other. He could smell her soft perfume on his skin as her breath touched his face. Her passion was overflowing and so was his. Two souls who found each other, kissed at the very park Cassie loved to visit. Lovers who declared their love, giving a promise to last forever. It didn't matter how long they knew each other before knowing; love happens when it's right. This was what Callen needed to bring back his smile, his heart was touched deeply by her presence. When he gazed into her hazel eyes he could imagine a family of children who looked just as beautiful. He could hear leaves rustling in the trees and her hair gently blew around her face and neck. They couldn't stop looking at one another. He looked at her hands. He held her hand up to mirror his and pressed them together. Then she interlaced her fingers with his. He was so happy he wanted to cry. She was still wearing the locket her father gave her when she turned five. It shimmered in the setting sunlight. This was their world, where only two people existed. They were in love.

"I don't know what to say," Cassie sighed.

"You don't have to say anything. Just let the sounds of the park be our music. I don't want to be without you."

"I wish my father were here. He'd love to meet you," Cassie longed.

"Would you like to meet my family?"

"Of course, I would."

"We could go to my house. You'll love my mom. She can cook anything you like."

"Can we go now?"

"Why not! Let's go!"

Callen didn't care about anything else at that moment. What he had was better than the times he was with Kate. In the moment, all was forgotten, his leg, his trauma, the rift with Charles. This was to be Cassie's day. He wanted nothing but to see her happy.

Walking up to his parents' house, he let Cassie enter first.

"Mom, Dad!" he shouted from behind her.

"Callen, what is it?" Mary asked.

"I want you all to meet someone. This is Cassie Adams."

"Hello, Cassie. It's nice to meet you. I'm Mary."

"Callen's told me so much about you and your cooking," Cassie smiled and looked back at Callen.

"Well, he has a big appetite."

The family gathered in the backyard. Charles heard everyone outside and came out to meet Cassie.

"Hey, Dad. Glad you could join us," Callen said.

"Nice to meet you. I'm Charles."

Sam stayed in the pool while the family visited. Cassie loved to talk about her father and why she loved school. Callen sat next to his father, wishing they could communicate like Cassie's dad.

"Callen, Garrett called. He wants you to call him," Mary remembered.

"Excuse me everyone. I'll see what he wants."

"Hey, Garrett, you called?"

"Yes. Kate and I want you and Cassie to come over for dinner. Are you open tomorrow?"

"I'll see if she's free. We're at the parents' house."

"How's that going?"

"Good. Dad joined us for a conversation. I still want him to understand me now that I have a girlfriend. Cassie and I just told each other that we are in love."

"Congratulations Callen. That's awesome. I think Dad would want you happy."

"I'll let you know if we can make it. I think Cassie would like to come with me."

They all sat around the outside fire talking and swapping stories. Cassie had such a beautiful laugh. As she talked, Callen watched her features dance in the firelight. He never thought he would love anyone this much. She fit into his world. Yet in his mind, he wasn't sure how he was going to explain his trauma to her. Being disabled used to scare him. Suddenly he saw his world looking differently because of her. With or without his father's approval, Callen was going to be alright with Cassie by his side.

# Chapter 12

Maddy was preoccupied with the floral shop. She had been thinking about what she would say when Daryl came to see his children. She just got a shipment of lavender colored Roses. It was a special order for an event coming up soon. She was unwrapping them when the phone rang. She wondered who would be calling after closing time.

"Hello."

"Madeline, it's Daryl."

"Why are you calling me at work?"

"I didn't want to write. I want to come and see the kids in two days. My flight is scheduled."

"You haven't given me much notice. Why the rush?"

"There's no rush. It seems like you just keep putting it off."

"How am I supposed to feel about you coming back into my life after nine years? The boys don't know you. To them you are just a stranger."

"If they get to know me, I can be their father again."

"Is that the real reason why you want to suddenly be in their lives?"

"Do you think it's because I want to get back with you? You made that perfectly clear. I'm okay with that."

"I've told them you want to meet them."

"And Kate? Have you told her?"

"She knows. But she might see you."

"I'm not a bad guy, Madeline."

"I never said that. You ran out on us without a word, a phone call, a letter. You left me with no means of supporting these children. Maybe you should have had a conversation with me and let me know that you were unhappy."

"At the time, I thought you would complicate matters by making me stay."

"Oh now this is my fault?"

"No, that's not what I'm saying. Look, if you don't let me see them, there are courts that can settle this."

"We promised each other we wouldn't do that. Don't threaten me with that now."

"Let me see them. I'll be there in two days. I'll call you when I land in California. Goodbye, Madeline."

Maddy didn't say anything. She hung up the phone thinking how she was going to prepare her children for this. She was angry at Daryl for waiting all these years to be a father. Walking back to the storage room, she put the flowers in the cooler. She thought it would be better to finish the order tomorrow. She had more important things to deal with at home.

Maddy walked into her home exhausted. Her conversation with Daryl made her mind tired, thinking of his visit.

"You're home a little earlier than usual. Are you okay?" Rosy asked.

"I'm okay. How are the boys doing?"

"They tried skipping homework. But that's just boys. But old Rosy is on the job. They can't put anything over on this babysitter."

Daryl called me at work. He mentioned court."

"I thought that wasn't an issue."

"I thought that too, but he is going to see them no matter what I do."

"What did he say?"

"He's arriving in two days."

"You did prepare the boys for this. I mean, you knew this was coming."

"I did tell them he wanted to see them. How do you get them to know a stranger who is also their father?"

"I think you will figure it out. The best thing is to keep an open line of communication with them."

"I need to chat with them tonight after dinner. Thanks again for watching them."

Maddy said goodbye to Rosy and started to prepare dinner.

"Hey, Mom. Can we go out to eat dinner?" asked Cody.

"Yeah, please Mom. We want pizza."

"Mom is very tired tonight. We can go out another day."

"Mom, Kate called. She wants you to call her back," said Cody.

"Okay. Did you finish your homework?"

"We finished. Rosy made us. Come on Chase, let's go outside until dinner's ready."

Maddy slid the dish in the oven and picked up the phone.

"Hello Kate. How are you doing?"

"Good."

"I wanted to talk to you about Daryl's visit."

"Do we have to talk about this?"

"Yes. I've been thinking about it. I realized that you were only doing what you thought was best."

"I'm glad you understand. Thanks Mom."

"Kate it's very hard for me to see your dad. It must be harder for you. I'm glad we're talking this through because your dad will be here in two days. He's flying in."

"Two days?"

"Kate, if you want to you can hear him out. I don't want to see him but there is not much at this point I can do about it."

"If I did, it would be for you. Maybe all I need is closure. I'm not sure if I will ever be close to him."

After dinner Maddy told the boys about their father. They seemed to be alright with it. She was a protective mother. All she wanted was the best for her children. She tried not to have anxiety about Daryl possibly taking her to court. She was a good mother, and she knew she wasn't going to lose her boys.

Daryl called to say his plane landed and rented a car to drive up. She told him to meet her at her place of business. It was a stressful two days since they last talked. She kept looking out the window, wondering what he looked like after all these years. Would she even recognize him? She wasn't going to get trapped into starting another relationship with him. To her this was simply business about their kids.

As she looked out, she saw a car parking against the curb. A tall man got out dressed in a camel hair coat. He was wearing sunglasses and a black outfit. He walked across the street. Taking off his sunglasses, his face was very handsome. For an older man, he still had good looks. Maddy opened the door to her floral shop.

"Hello, Daryl."

"Madeline. It's so good to see you."

"I wish I could say the same."

"I was prepared for you to say that."

"I don't want you to go to my home until we talk first."

"I'm impressed you own a business."

"I'm capable of taking care of my family even if you weren't part of it."

"Can we lay off the sarcasm? There's no need for hostility. I'm trying to work it out with you."

"By threatening to take me to court?"

"I apologize for that."

"I never said you can't see them. Your life is in New York. How are you going to see them if you live there?"

"I thought about that. Maybe I could move here."

"Really? Well, it's sunny California and you are dressed in a coat like you are having drinks at The Plaza in the Winter."

"I'm just trying to think of a way to get closer to them."

Maddy was trying to keep her cool at this point. She was frustrated. She didn't want him to move here and disrupt her routine and her life.

She decided to cut to the point.

"Let's talk about what you want out of this."

"I lost the woman I loved and my son. There has been an emptiness in my heart that aches. It made me miss my children. I made some stupid choices and from what I can see you haven't forgiven me yet."

"If you could see into my world, you would know what I went through when you left. It was awful and very difficult."

"I'm sure it was. I can't go back and fix what I did. I was a good husband to Annie. I changed into a better person. She made it possible for me to be here right now to make things right with you."

"I'm sorry you lost them. Losing my sister Karen still hurts. I still have a scar on my heart from losing you. I really loved you. But that's over and in the past."

"I did love you too. I can't explain why I did what I did. Can we try to be civil about my visit without trying to hurt each other?"

"I think we can."

Maddy and Daryl talked about what each of them expected from the visit. He was staying at hotel for three days. It was going to be hard to get to know the children in just a few days.

"You can meet me at my home tomorrow."

"You said the boys are in Little League. I bought them some new gloves and baseballs. I hope they like them."

"They will. They're good boys."

Maddy came home, telling the boys their father was in town. She urged them to get some sleep if they were going to be ready for the next day.

Daryl showed up early the next morning with a box full of stuff. Maddy let him in, nervous about him entering her safe home.

"We can have a seat here. The boys will be down soon."

"This is a beautiful home."

"It was Karen's."

"I remember when she and Michael went to New Jersey with us after we got married. She always wore a hat and covered up at the beach. You loved being in the ocean." Daryl smiled when he mentioned that memory. "We were different, but we loved each other."

Maddy didn't give a response to that comment. The boys came running down the stairs, wearing the clothes Maddy picked out for them to wear.

"Daryl, I'd like you to meet your sons."

"Hi there. You have grown. It's nice to see you."

"Are you really our dad?" probed Chase.

"Yes. I thought we could get to know each other better."

"Are those presents for us?"

"Oh, yes. It's some baseball stuff."

The boys opened the gifts and thanked him. They ran outside to try out the new gloves.

"Madeline, they're beautiful. I can see Chase looks like you. Do you have any pictures of Katharine?"

"I have her wedding album."

Maddy handed the album to Daryl. He went through the pages touching Kate's face on the photo.

"I have missed so much. My Katharine. She's so beautiful. She looks happy."

"She wasn't happy before we moved here."

"She was such a lovely bride."

"She still hasn't fully decided to see you."

"I'm sure our meeting wouldn't be easy," Daryl admitted.

"No, it wouldn't be. She's still skeptical about you. She was so hurt when you left. I think that was why she got into so much trouble."

Daryl felt bad about how much Kate went through. He was the father who left his daughter scarred.

She would always remember Garrett's promise to love, keep her safe, and cared for. She would never worry that he would hurt their children by leaving. Kate didn't want to see her father because she knew it would bring back the pain of how much she loved him. The pain of not hearing a goodbye. It was as if she turned around and he was gone after she built her world around him. She was left without the man whom she dreamed would walk her down the aisle. She never expected him to do something so despicable and selfish. Kate wanted to love her father again, but she held back. What if he hurt her or her mother again? Kate didn't want to be disrespectful. She was disappointed in him, and she was allowed her thoughts.

Daryl watched the boys play in the backyard and felt heavy in his heart.

I"I thought all these years about what I did. I questioned my motives and hated myself for so long. I went through depression from abandoning my family."

"I don't believe you need to be punished anymore. It's been nine years. You've gone through loss. Being here with the boys can help you move on. These boys are your family regardless of what we've both been through. Let's agree that we will not involve courts when it comes to the boys. Can you do that?"

Maddy was trying to keep it together by being understanding.

"Okay. You have my word on that. Can I talk to them. You can sit with us if you'd like."

"Sure."

Daryl called out to the boys. He had them sit with their parents.

"How do you boys feel about me being here?" Daryl asked.

"I don't remember you. Why did you go away?"

"Well, I wasn't thinking very clear at the time. I made a bad mistake. I want us to be friends. What do you think about that?"

"It's kinda weird you want us to be your friend and you're our dad. How are you going to visit us if you live in New York?" asked Cody.

"We can figure that out later. We can take it slow and just get to know each other."

"What about Kate?" asked Chase.

"Your sister likes to go by Kate?"

"We haven't called her Katharine for a long time," informed Chase.

"I'd like to see Kate. You can ask me anything. I will try to answer any questions you have about me."

"Are you staying for dinner?" asked Chase.

"I don't know if your mom wants me to stay."

"No, not at this time, boys."

The boys threw the ball out back with their dad. They asked him the usual questions when getting to know someone new.

"Maybe I should have dressed more appropriate for a playing ball," said Daryl.

"You look like you're going to a party," said Chase.

"I'll wear jeans and a T-shirt tomorrow."

Maddy was a little more relaxed seeing the boys get to know Daryl. Even though she no longer loved him, she felt like they were almost a family again. She loved that her children don't handle issues like adults. The boys liked him and didn't mind spending time with him.

The evening ended and Daryl wanted to talk to Maddy outside of the house by the front door.

"Madeline, thank you for a nice evening. It felt good to be a dad again. If you knew my son Connor, you would have loved him." He teared up, "This means so much to me."

"They like you."

"I'd like to see Kate tomorrow. Can you call her?"

"I can call her."

"Thank you. See you tomorrow."

She went back inside noticing Daryl's car lights from the window. The boys were doing the dishes as asked. Maddy went into the kitchen to help out.

"Did you boys have fun?"

"He's nice. We had fun. We like the baseball gloves."

"Would you like him to come over more?"

"I guess it would be okay," said Cody.

Maddy was thinking about Kate. The abandonment had more of an impact on her than the boys. How much resentment and pain was she harboring? Maddy felt it was Kate's right to navigate her choice as she felt. She was an adult who made her own decisions.

Maddy spoke to Kate that night, and she agreed to meet Daryl at the park.

Kate arrived at the park early, reflecting on what she would say. She thought about what Garrett had said. He encouraged her to give him a chance to speak. She was biting her lip assuming it would not end well. She wanted to scream at the man who left his family, who left them to struggle for years. How could that be forgiven? Kate immediately stood up and ran to her car. It was better to be at Garrett's side while she felt that strongly. Kate didn't think Daryl deserved an explanation. He did the same thing to her. If she let her father back into her life, she would get hurt and he would just leave her all over again. She had a good thing going with Garrett. She didn't want any more pain from Daryl in the future. She would protect her heart and her family. Kate drove away never to see Daryl again.

A white car passed her as she drove home. It was Daryl. He waited there at the park for Kate. After a half hour he began thinking. What he had done to his daughter was made clear. Did she do it to get even? She obviously no longer needed him in her life. She was happy, loved, and satisfied without him. Daryl felt very low about her rejection. He was going to move on from it and no longer try to contact Kate. It was hard to accept. He was left alone by his only daughter. As he got back in his car, he slowly drove back to Maddy's to see his boys.

"Kate never showed up," Daryl said quietly.

"Well, think about how hard it's been for her. You did break her heart."

"Why wouldn't she give me a chance?"

"How could you ask that? You did the same thing to us."

"I guess I deserved that."

"You may to have to live without her in your life. She's very happy with herself. She did that on her own."

"She became that way because of you."

"She may have your stubborn ways, but she manages to hold it together very well."

"I wanted to know if I can take the boys to the beach."

"Not by yourself. I can come for a couple of hours. This visit is between you and me."

"You really think I'm that stupid to kidnap them?"

"I don't know much about you. As long as you are here to see them, I make the rules. Fair enough?"

"I get it. There's nothing wrong with you coming along."

While at the beach, they didn't laugh together or act like the couple they used to be. They were only parents to their boys. Kate was now out of his family picture. The boys flew their new kites in the breeze, they splashed in the shoreline, and built sand castles with their parents. Maddy and Daryl said little to each other. She too was keeping herself emotionally safe. Soon Daryl would be out of her life and on his way home to New York.

That evening, Daryl said his goodbye to his sons. The visit with his boys was special to him. Maddy had an idea that he might never return to see them. She was right. He never contacted or came to see the boys again. After Kate refused to see him, he knew the pain would return if he did. Daryl went on with his life and Maddy never learned anything more about him. Since then, no one has heard from Daryl Parker.

# Chapter 13

It had been six months since Daryl's visit. The boys asked about him one other time but never again after that.

Kate enjoyed creating more books. Her friend knew a publisher who was interested in talking to Kate about her books. She was now getting her confidence back after letting her father go. It felt good to be strong enough to become her bravest. Kate still thought about wanting a baby, but she preferred to write until she felt ready. She talked to the publisher on the phone and made an appointment to submit her manuscripts for review. This was a big step for Kate. Garrett always supported her and motivated her to be a gifted author. She was a natural in her writings. She put down the emotion, heart, and warmth in her lines. Her penned romance was sensual and tender. In the past, she never thought she was good at it. She was afraid to read her own manuscripts and many times she tossed them in the trash. She was inspired by her husband to write romantic words of love. He was a kind and gentle lover to her. He knew how she liked to be kissed. She loved to hold his strong hands and be playful at the same time. Somedays, just sitting on the porch swing, holding him was all she needed. Kate avoided subjects with fear and pain. She already experienced enough of that in her past. She used parts of her life and her relationship with Garrett to paint the picture of what real love was. Kate was now feeling like a true author, a writer who could go far with her books to touch the hearts of her readers.

"Kate Carrington, Mr. Brice will see you now," the receptionist said.

"Kate, it's nice to meet you." He held his hand out.

"Thank you for having an interest in my books."

"Kate, we read your manuscripts. They are phenomenal. We think you would be a perfect candidate for our list of gifted authors. We would like to publish some of your books. We will take them to our editors, and we can meet to choose covers, and get them out to the public."

"Wow, this is fantastic news!"

"We wished you could have contacted us sooner. You are a wonderful writer."

"I wished that too. My husband encouraged me to keep on."

"Well, we're glad you are publishing with us. Congratulations."

"Thank you, Mr. Brice."

Kate couldn't believe she was going to fulfill her dream. Kate Carrington; Author. Years of hard work and wishing came true for the girl who made friends with sadness and loneliness in New York City. She came to life when she met Garrett. He was her biggest help in making her life bright again.

Garrett came home and could hear Kate's typewriter tapping in the background. He was working on a special project out of town that left him very dirty and dusty. He went out back to rinse off his dirty face and arms. Kate could hear him, and she went out to see him. She watched him rinsing cool water through his hair.

"You know, I remember looking at you do that at the nursery when you took me there for the first time."

"I knew you were staring," he smiled.

"Really, are you trying to impress me right now?"

"Sure. Do you want me to come in the house dirty?"

"No, I'll get you a towel."

As she turned around Garrett ran over and grabbed her from behind.

"No need to do that. I'll just do this."

"Garrett, you're getting me wet and dirty," she said in a playful manner.

"Who needs a towel when I have you."

"Oh, I have some news. You're going to love this," said Kate as she handed him a towel.

"Now that I'm dry, let's hear it."

"My friend Liza gave me the phone number to a publishing company. Well, Dak Brice loved my books. They are going to publish me."

"Honey, that's great! I knew you could do it!"

"I was working on a new story when you came home."

"I love that sound when I come home."

"I have dinner in the crock pot. Please, go take a real shower and get ready to eat."

"So this isn't good enough?"

"No. Love you."

Kate wouldn't give up this life for anything. She was in the best place. She loved taking time to go with Garrett to his landscape projects and always learned something about trees and shrubbery. He was at his crowning factor. She learned how to take care of her own garden and sometimes would teach anyone the botany she picked up. It was amazing how far she had come. She was great at her trade, writing and landscaping. She knew she could do anything to keep up her emotional strength in any situation. She was also realistic, realizing she could faulter and fail. It was nothing like the times before. She had the power to make her dreams come true.

# Chapter 14

Callen was accepted to study mathematics at the university. He and Cassie were promised to each other. He informed her of his need for therapy to deal with his PTSD and anxiety. She did what she could to help him get better. He finally received an appointment with the orthopedic surgeon about improving his knee function.

"Well, doctor what do you think? Can I ditch the cane anytime soon?"

"Callen, you could have stopped using it a long time ago. The injury has healed quite well. You still need to strengthen those muscles. You don't need the cane."

"I have weakness and pain when I try not to use it."

"I understand, but you will improve faster without it. You are going to have to exercise your leg to get it strong again."

"I don't need any more surgeries?"

"No. You have a little inflammation under the kneecap. That might be causing the discomfort. I'll make the appointment for you to go to physical therapy twice a week."

"Thank you, Doctor. That's great news."

"Callen, leave the cane."

"Doctor, I'd like to take it with me. My brother and I agreed to burn it together. I won't use it."

"Very well. Make sure you don't give in. It won't strengthen you."

"Okay."

Callen walked out of the office limping, still fearing the pain returning when walking. He knew he no longer needed the crutch to help him deal with the pain. He felt like this was a metaphor that was related to him and his father. Callen came home to see his father. Since he introduced Cassie they visited often, and they warmed up to her easily. He could see that they loved her as a part of their own family. It made him feel better. In his heart, he loved his father very much. He lost hope in their relationship, failing to compromise many times. He might give it another try.

"Hey, Dad."

"Callen, where's your cane?"

"The doctor said I no longer needed it. I have to walk without it. I'm sure I'll get used to it."

"It's good to see you walking without it."

"Dad, can we talk? I don't want to talk over old issues."

"What are you trying to say?"

"I wanted to tell you that I love you. I know you want what's best for me and I'm a man who can take care of himself."

"I know you can. As a father, I want you to make good choices. In the past you didn't."

"I know. I was wrong. I have been seeing a specialist to help me with my PTSD and the nightmares I've been experiencing. I'm feeling a little better."

"I'm glad you're getting help. I never could have imagined going through that like you did."

"How do you feel about Cassie?"

"She's lovely, son."

"She's my family. Dad, I love her. I want her to be my wife. In the years to come, I want you to be proud of what I overcame."

"I am proud of you. You are going to make a wonderful husband. I wish I could have set a better example for you and your brothers."

"We're here now and everything is alright. We need to get back to us again. I want my dad in my life. I want to do things with you. I want to have conversations with you."

"That makes my heart feel good. As I age, it gets harder to stay alert. I grow more tired every day and I wish I didn't have these wrinkles."

"Dad, you'll be around for a long time. You're going to be a grandpa someday. You will always have this family to love."

"I'm not the kind of person to show much emotion. I should have been that way. I feel selfish."

"We've all had those moments. It's best not to rehash them."

Callen walked over to his father and put his hand on his shoulder. Charles reached around to hold him. Both were filled with emotions that were long overdue. A gentle hug pulled them together.

"I don't know where I would be if you weren't here, Callen. I was afraid death was going to claim you and I would never get the opportunity to tell you what you mean to me."

"I've moved on from that, Dad. I'm going to have a happy life with Cassie. Live every moment like it was our last."

"Callen, do you remember when we felt like we had a second chance to have a happy life together? I couldn't come back from the fear I was going through. Now I see that I can."

They began to see things through each other's eyes. Both were going through sadness and fear that kept them from being close.

Even though Kate and Callen never had a romantic future together, she came to his side and without judging him. Kate became his rescuer until Cassie appeared. Callen was going to have the life he always wanted. That would include having a dad he could be friends with. It wasn't too late for Sam to learn from his family. He was going to have the chance to have a good family and happy life.

"Hello, is Garrett there?"

"No, he's out buying peat moss. What do you need?"

"Um, I wanted to talk to him about Cassie."

"Are you guys getting serious?"

"Maybe."

"And you want your brother to help you with romance, a landscaper? Why wouldn't you ask a romance writer to help you?"

"You mean, you would help me?"

"Are you going to propose?"

"I am."

"Did you talk to her mother about this?"

"I talked to her an hour ago. She was happy for Cassie."

Kate suggested they meet the afternoon of Cassie's Sunday family dinner. Kate used her mother's key to open the florist shop. It was fragrant.

"Mom said to make a list of what we will use for inventory. The Roses are over here. She likes pink Roses? Here are the different shades of pink ones."

They created a bouquet of fourteen pink Roses and placed a white one in the center. Inside the white petals he tied the ring.

He held it up to admire, "Do you think she will say yes to this?"

"She can't say no."

Callen asked Cassie to marry him that evening and she accepted in front of her family.

With careful planning and some time, Callen and Cassie married in front of friends and family in her mother's backyard. Garrett watched his brother come up out of his despair and stand by his side without a cane, and his past behind him. Charles wanted to walk Cassie down the aisle. It was an honor to do this for Callen.

Callen and Cassie managed marriage and school simultaneously. Callen worked part time as a CPA to provide for his wife. They lived in a tiny apartment, living a simple life together. Callen loved being married. It was like a having a best friend beside him every day. He wanted to give Cassie a secure and loving future.

Maddy had been looking through the letters Daryl had sent. She was over his neglect and selfishness and was smart enough to know he would never change. She gave him the benefit of the doubt. That may have been a way for her to close the book on that chapter of her life. It looked like Daryl was gone for good. At the time, she couldn't completely shut him out. If he wanted to, he could have hired a good attorney and sent her to court for custody. Each year without a letter was relieving. His words became ashes, thoughts that were burned into smoke. They were not worth treasuring or keeping; just a reminder that no one should try to steal her power. Her boys were going to grow up fine young men who made it through some tough years. They would learn how to securely care for a family. They had the support of their mother and sister. Maddy was resilient, strong, and capable of coming back from the pain inflicted. She felt that he was gone for the time, and she could resume her happy routine.

Kate remembered the day she left her father alone wait-ing for her. It wasn't cold-hearted. She wanted him to feel what it was like to be abandoned by someone she cared for. She felt low enough about herself back when he first left. A daughter was shattered, left in the rain without the father she loved so dear. He appeared heartless, uncar-ing, and selfish. Kate knew those words were harsh, but she also knew anyone who did what he did was not a kind person. For most people, leaving the past behind was a hard thing to overcome. Kate, when she lived in New York, had a poor, modest life that blossomed into some-thing beautiful when she met Garrett. She saw new beauty in natural things. The mountains, rivers, streams, and most of all, the trees gave her a reason to trust her life was going to be what she dreamed of. Kate had clo-sure. She was focused on her family and all the new ad-ditions to the Carrington household. It was now time for Kate to begin achieving goals she wanted to accomplish all her life. She was going to be a renowned writer. She looked forward to having a fanbase of readers enjoy her talent.

Kate had hopes for her growing family, too. For the first time, she had the strength to go into what would have been her baby's room. Her breath was taken away as she observed the things awaiting her inside. The crib, the mo-bile over the bed, the wallpaper she put up, and the changing table filled and all the needs for a newborn. Kate knew it was time to be a mom again. Looking out the window, she noticed the tree Garrett planted and how it was growing and thriving. She wanted to be like that tree. She thought about where she was just a few years ago. Her family had grown. Kate and Callen were now in different places in their lives. Taking time to let things heal was just what Kate needed to become ready to start a family with Garrett. Kate had a secret. She was pregnant and Garrett didn't know. She had known for a few weeks but didn't want to tell Garrett for fear that she could have another miscarriage. She felt ready to give the man she loved life-changing news. They were going to be Carrington three. Kate had new life growing inside her. She was told that her baby was healthy and doing well. Kate and Garrett would finally embark on a journey of becoming parents.

Garrett walked by the nursery and realized that the door was left open.

"Kate!"

"Yes, love."

"The door is open. I mean the baby's room door. Was that you?"

She neared him, grabbed his hand, and pulled him into the nursery.

"You are smiling, Kate. What's going on?"

"We are."

"You mean ...?"

"Yes. We are going to have another little landscaper in the family."

# Chapter 15

Kate stood near their citrus tree in the sunlight wearing her laced summer dress. She was radiant and beautiful as Garrett watched her. The days had been so pleasant and being outside was Kate's favorite pastime. Garrett went inside the house to answer the phone. It was Mary and she was crying.

"Mom, what's wrong?"

"It's your father. Garrett, he died twenty minutes ago. He was walking to the backyard, and he collapsed. I called the paramedics, but they couldn't revive him."

"What?"

"I'm so sorry, Son. There was nothing anyone could have done to stop it from happening."

Charles had not been feeling well. He was tired and had not eaten much for the day. He had been feeling some pain in his chest but just ignored it. He kept thinking about Mary and how much he loved her and his children. Charles' heart was full toward those he held dear. Mary and Charles had talked over how Charles handled his relationship with Callen. He realized that time was short, and family should mean everything to him.

"Mary, I'm sorry about how I have been feeling. I know this is long overdue, but I want to appreciate my son again."

"I know you do. It seems like things have been going on this way for so long. We're not getting any younger and our boys are married men who will probably bring us some beautiful grandchildren."

"Callen mentioned that too. I look forward to enjoying having them over."

"Me too. Come on, let's get some tea and sit outside, just the two of us," Mary encouraged.

Charles got up to go meet her by the lawn chairs when he felt his chest tighten. He had a hard time breathing and couldn't call for Mary. She came out to be with the glasses and found him lying on the ground.

"Charles, Charles! Oh no, Charles," she cried out.

She knew that he was gone, and this conversation would be her last with the man she loved and cared for. Now she could do nothing to save him. She held him in her arms until the paramedics arrived. When they came, she couldn't let him go. It was heartbreaking for the medics to see her in such pain. Mary was now a widow and Sam would grow up without his father.

"Where's Sam?"Garrett said. "Have you told Callen?"

"Sam is with Rosy. Callen doesn't know yet."

"I don't know what to do with this. Mom, help me know what to do," Garrett panicked.

"I don't know what to do either. I still can't believe my husband is gone."

"Let me tell Callen, please, Mom."

"Alright, Garrett. I'm going to book a flight to my sister's for a couple of days. I'm taking Sam with me. I need to see her and talk about funeral arrangements."

Mary began to cry harder. She loved Charles. She was able to see her husband change his ways and it came too soon that he would leave her and their boys.

"Where is Callen?" Garrett asked.

"I'm not sure of anything right now, son."

"I'll go talk to him. I love you, Mom. This is hard but we are going to be ok."

"I love you. I'll call you when I leave."

Hanging up that phone felt like the heaviest weight for Garrett. No one close to him had ever died before. He and his family were just starting to have their best relationship with Charles. They mended several family issues and were on their way to being whole again. This news was devastating, and he slowly went outside to talk to Kate.

"I think we are going to have a good crop this year. Look at these buds. Garrett what's wrong? Who called?"

"It was my mother. My father passed away a few minutes ago. I think he had a heart attack again."

"Oh no. Garrett, how is your mother?"

"She's going to stay at Aunt Becky's in Rhode Island for a couple of days. Sam is going with her."

Garrett came to Kate as they both cried, and he held her tightly.

"Kate, I loved my dad. I loved him. I just got him back and he's gone.'

"I know, baby. I hurt too. I'm so sorry."

"I have to go see Callen."

"He doesn't know?"

"No. I want to be the one to tell him."

"You should go. I'll be okay here."

Garrett's emotions grew deeper while driving to Callen's. He knew his brother's anxieties could resurface if the news was too much. Garrett was trying to find the right way to tell him. Callen and his father had just started understanding each other and Callen planned his future around him. Stopping his truck in the driveway, Garrett took a deep breath and he stepped out. He was nervous as he walked up to the door.

"Garrett, what are you doing here? Something wrong?"

"Yes. Callen, I need to talk to you."

"Come on in. Cassie went out for the day."

"I got a call from Mom."

"Garrett, just say it. Is it Dad?"

"Yes. He collapsed in the backyard, and he died about an hour ago."

"What are you talking about?'

"Callen..."

"No! Did you just tell me Dad is dead?"

"Callen, I'm sorry."

"Sorry, you're sorry? Is that supposed to make me feel better?"

"I know this is hard. I'm not handling it right either. He was my father too."

"You don't understand. We were doing good. He was finally coming around to be my father. I've waited my whole life to have that and now he's gone? He left me. I need to see Mom."

"She's on her way to see her sister. She'll be gone for a few days. She needs it to help her makes sense of everything."

Callen cried on the couch as Garrett watched his brother fall to pieces.

"Callen, do you want me to stay here with you? You can come home with me, Kate is there. Please, just don't be alone with this."

"No, I need to do something. I need to know Mom is okay."

"She is. Let her go away. I don't think she can be in the house right now."

"Garrett, I can't be without my father. He was becoming part of my life. I just told him he will be around for a long time. Why is he gone, Garrett?"

Garrett went over to hold him as the brothers wept together. The loss they felt was a shock to this family who felt like love was back in their lives. Callen agreed to come home with Garrett until Cassie returned.

"I know Dad wanted to mend things with you, Callen. At least, you two made up before he died."

"It wasn't supposed to be this way. He was supposed to go on trips with us, spend time with grandkids, and just spend time with us."

"I wanted that too. When Mom gets home, we need to help her too," Garrett said as he held back tears.

The men got out of the truck and Kate ran into Garrett's arms. Kate could see Callen wasn't taking it very well. His eyes were red. She reached out for him and held him as he sobbed.

"Do you want me to call Cassie and tell her where you are?" Kate suggested.

"I'll try to see if she's at her mother's."

Callen made the call and contacted Cassie.

"Can we meet somewhere? I don't want to go home," admitted Callen.

"Why, what's wrong, Callen?"

"I'll tell you when I see you. Can you meet me at the park with the bridge?"

Close by was a beautiful area with a walk that bridged the water surrounded by weeping willows and eucalyptus. Callen had his brother drop him off.

Cassie met found him sitting on the bench with his head in his hands.

"Okay, Callen. Please tell me why we can't go home."

"My father died today at home."

"Oh my, Callen, I'm so sorry. How is your mom doing?"

"She's leaving to see her sister with Sam. She can't go home right now. I guess I feel just like her."

"Honey, I know how you feel."

"What? Did you say you know how I feel? You had a relationship that was good with your dad. I didn't. Please don't try to say you understand."

"That's not what I meant. What am I supposed to say? I was just trying to be supportive. Please don't be upset at me."

"No one knows how this feels for me. I believed we were going to be okay. He was coming around to really loving me. I lost that chance."

"What can I do?"

"Nothing. No one can do anything. I will never get that opportunity to have him watch me grow into someone he always wanted in his life."

"These things always take time to heal. You will be there for the rest of your family."

"I'm afraid to go home. I'm already anxious and I don't think I can sleep tonight."

"You have me, Callen. I'll be there for you. We can stay at Garrett and Kate's house. Right now, let's just sit here and rest."

Callen could feel the nurturing he received from Cassie. She was a good comfort for him. It was nice to be around family during difficult times.

Mary landed in Rhode Island with Sam by her side. Mary's sister Becky picked her up from the airport. Together, they would gain some sense about her options.

"I'm so happy you're here. I've got the room fixed up for you and Sam."

"Thank you Becky, for seeing us on short notice."

"It's more than fine, sis. I hope I can help."

They talked about memories, old times when Mary first met Charles. He was older than her, looking so mature while Mary felt like a teenager in her heart. They married when Mary was just close to twenty years old. Charles was thirty-three.

Becky helped with the life insurance and made suggestions to help Mary lessen her stress.

"Have you thought about selling the house? I mean, it's just a thought," Becky suggested.

"I don't know. I bought that house with Charles. We have so many memories tied up there."

"I'm not sure if you can take care of the house. You and Sam may be able to get something smaller, easier to maintain."

"I just can't think about that yet."

"Okay. I just want to help."

"I know."

Mary went to bed that night. She felt strange sleeping alone without her love next to her. She couldn't stay asleep. She went into the kitchen to get some water. Sam heard her.

"Mom, why are you up?"

"Oh, hi dear. I can't sleep."

"I miss Dad. I started to cry but I stopped because Dad would want me to be brave."

"Honey, it's okay to cry. Dad wouldn't have minded. How are you feeling about all this?"

"I'm sad. I know Dad had times when we didn't see him much. I really thought I would get time with him. He told me he wanted to take a trip with me and my brothers. He had planned what we were going to do together. I want that back."

"I didn't know you talked with him about that. That sounds like it would have been fun. Maybe you could do something like that with your brothers."

"It won't be the same."

"No, it won't. But we're still a family. We have to help each other get through this. We will try together."

"I'd like that."

"Did you know your father named you?"

"He did?"

"Yes. He always wanted a son named Sam. His great-grandfather's name was Samuel."

"I didn't know that."

They talked for an hour about some of the things Sam never knew about his father. Mary bonded with Sam that night. It didn't matter that they lost sleep. This was an important moment to gain support from the woman who shaped his life. That time would benefit him later in life, learning to be a good man by remembering good advice from a good mother.

Mary knew Charles' father died from heart disease at a young age. When he had his last heart attack, Mary was afraid that it could be his last. She had just connected with her husband. She got through to him and she was on her way to having a satisfying life together with their older children. Her plans had changed abruptly, and she was uneasy about living alone. She was going to go slow with this. She was in no hurry to get over Charles passing any time soon. Mary grieved for a few months when her mother died. It was not easy for her to say goodbye to those who she dearly loved. She was strong, but not strong enough to move on quickly. Sam would be well-taken care of. She never had a hard time focusing on him and his needs. They were Mother and Son, getting through the death of someone they would never forget, Charles Callen Carrington.

# Chapter 16

Everyone who loved the Carrington family came to Charles' funeral. It was a memorial service that honored and celebrated the good times Charles had with his family. Mary and her children sat in the front and each one got to say something about their father, about a good memory to treasure.

"Hello, everyone. I'm happy we are all here today, but I wish it were on better terms. My father loved this family. He worked two jobs before I was born to be sure we were comfortable and fed. I remember when we lived in Florida, he tried surfing. He fell off that surfboard so many times, but he was determined to ride a wave. After many attempts, he finally got up. That was how he was in real life. He never gave up on any of us and he wanted the best for his family. He had his moments when he was difficult to understand, but we still respected him. My father had the chance to see his children grow and marry. He grew old with his wife and loved her very much. Me and my brothers learned so much from him. He is going to be missed and we as a family will carry on his legacy. Thank you."

Callen was invited to say a few words, but he couldn't. He wanted to remember Charles as the father who made the effort to try and love his son. That was a big loss for him, and no one sensed what he was feeling inside...except Kate. Even Cassie felt like she couldn't reach him. After the funeral, Kate walked over to where Callen was sitting alone.

"Hey, why are you here by yourself?"

"I don't want to socialize. I want to honor him alone. I want that privilege."

"You can have that. You don't have to be so brave. Grieving is usually about healing with time."

"Time just means I'm forgetting about him. I'd give anything to talk to him again. We had forgiven each other. We had plans, memories to make, and a future. Where do I go from here?"

"My father is alive, but it is as if he died when he left us. I carried that resentment for so long. I finally grew tired of the pain. It took time and I don't need him anymore. You lost someone you loved, and you will keep his memory even if time goes by. He would want you to heal on your own time."

"I know you're right. I just can't see it right now. You know, I like our relationship, Kate. We have a past with each other and now you are the sister I never had."

"Nothing changed with our friendship. I can see myself supporting you through your life. I will always be here."

"Cassie and I are trying to communicate with each other. She doesn't know what to do for me," he realized.

"Sometimes just being supportive is all you need. She is grieving too.'

"How's that?"

"She lost a father too. It won't be exactly the same for each of you, but this could be a recurring emotion with her. Losing a father has to be hard for her too."

"I was so wrapped up in my own feelings, I never thought about that."

"She's standing by that tree. Go over to her and let her know you appreciate her."

"I'm afraid to let her near me when I feel like this."

"Tell her that. You don't have say the perfect words. Just talk to her. She loves you and she wants you to come to her."

"Okay. Thank you, Kate."

"Callen, I really loved your father. I miss him too."

He just smiled and walked to Cassie. He didn't say a word. He just put his arms around her and held her. She welcomed that embrace. He could see she had been crying since she was feeling the memory of someone she loved. Cassie looked over her shoulder at Kate and whispered, "thank you."

Saying goodbye to Charles was something Mary wasn't prepared for. She put her hand on his casket and kissed the rose she put on it. Sam held his head down as his mother came to sit next to him.

"How are you, Sam?"

"I don't know. I want him back."

"I know. I want that too. You will never have to feel alone as long as you have me. We'll be okay. We just need time."

"What if I forget him?"

"You won't. I promise."

Everyone walked back to their cars and hugged the family. It was a time of reflection, thinking how one man shaped a family and supported his wife. No one thought of his flaws or how much he worked to curb his stresses. He was a distant man who was ignored as a child, pushed toward wealth and hard work to avoid making his father ashamed of him. In his heart he was a good man. He became kind, worthy, and forgiving. His children would not get to enjoy the man who came back from his sad place. He was too young to die, and it was unexpected. There was love in this family. In time, they would see generations sprout as new life entered into their world. Kate and Garrett would be the first ones to carry on Charles' legacy. An honor he would be proud of.

# Chapter 17

It had been six months since Charles passed away. Kate was almost ready to have her baby. She and Garrett wanted to be surprised. Was it a boy or a girl? Kate carried on the tradition of having fresh flowers in her home. She learned that from Karen. Garrett was sitting in the backyard after he raked up the dead leaves. Kate came to him putting her arms around his neck. He took her hand in his and held her belly. Bending over he put his cheek on it. She couldn't help but run her hands in his hair. Kate loved holding Garrett during those tender moments where she needed his attention. He knew the right time to hold her, kiss her, and just be by her side.

"What are you thinking about while you are out here?"

"I was thinking about you. It won't be long, and our child will be here. Probably running around out here. It's a beautiful thought," he envisioned.

"I'm happy and also sad."

"Sad? Why?"

"This will be over soon and I'm going to miss carrying this baby."

"Oh, Kate, we have so many good times ahead of us. Boy or girl, we are going to give this child so much love. We will be great parents."

"Garrett, how have you been? You're mom went back again to visit her sister. Do you think she'll move to Rhode Island?"

"I haven't asked her about that. She mentioned she might want to sell the house. It's paid for and she has no mortgage so selling it would help her out financially."

"It's probably not about money. She has to be ready for a big decision like that."

"I was going to visit her and talk about it after she returns."

"I would hate to have her move away and not see our baby."

"We'll wait to see what she thinks is best. I think we have time to put baby's crib together. It looks like it's going to take the two of us."

She was taking time off from writing to rest before the baby arrived. Her body was tiring more easily. Kate's publisher called her with good news about how her campaign.

"Hello, Mr. Brice. I'm so glad you called."

"Kate, congratulations on the new baby coming. Not long now, right? Are you ready for some good news?"

"Oh yes."

"Your books are selling at a fast pace. We have orders pouring in and your series is a hit. Hiring that marketing team was a great idea."

"Wow! That is great news. I have some new ideas for another book I have started on. I'm excited everyone loves my stories."

"We are very happy you are publishing with us. You have the potential to be a best seller."

"I never imagined I'd be on the best seller's list. I can't wait to tell Garrett."

"Well, you take it easy, and we hope to see a new novel after your little one is born. I'll be in touch if we hear more about your books."

"Thank you so much."

Kate couldn't believe what she just heard. She was a lonely girl, a troubled woman, and grew up without a father who didn't care. She lived in poverty and despair. Now she was going to be a mother and novelist. She would always remember the words of her mother, that she would get her reward someday. Kate worked hard to climb out of the fear and sadness she experienced. She looked back on her life with strength in her to change the course she was on. Being with Garrett and belonging to the Carrington family also made a difference in her life and demeanor.

Kate loved to write books about drama, and romance. She studied poetry and loved the flow of endearing words of love. She had been reading up on editing and English grammar.

She was a perfect example of a woman who became successful with persistence. She grew up around concrete and tall buildings. When she walked to school, she would see the girls who dressed in clothes she could only dream of wearing. She never had goals to be famous or have money. Writing was all she knew, and it was something she kept to herself. She believed she would never get to share her talent with anyone. The apartment she lived in with her brothers and mother was damp and smelled bad. She had to share a very small bathroom with her family and at times the plumbing didn't work. She didn't get to eat her favorite foods because of the amount of money her mother earned. Their refrigerator was small and broke down often. She was cold at night and slept with her brothers while her mother slept on the couch. When she thought about where she came from, she smiled. Her mother worked hard to care for them. Kate was happy she became like her and her aunt Karen. She wanted to be like her, not rich, but having her personality.

Kate experienced a love for landscapes, built and natural. She never saw trees so beautiful until Garrett introduced her. She loved the rustling sound, the shade they provided, the homes they made for animals and birds of every kind. She saw the tree as something she could pattern after. Tall, proud to stand, giving life to all who were in their presence. All her life, Kate wanted the life that would bring out who she really was, lovely at heart and capable of giving consideration to whoever crossed her path. She became kind and thoughtful. She learned to be nurturing, Garrett added to that. When Daryl left, he couldn't realize what he left behind. He missed the chance to love and get to know a beautiful woman who wanted nothing but to be loved.

Kate was Garrett's first love. Before her he never kissed a woman. Holding Kate in his arms was something that pleased his soul. Her skin and hair were beautiful, but when she smiled he could see that she was truly in love. They stayed in love, feeling the sensation of love's first kiss each time together. Kate still remembered the shy young man who loved natural things and painted landscapes using his imagination to create. He put his canvas art into real life when he met Kate. He also created a garden of serenity for her comfort. Kate wasn't just the landscaper's wife; she was a complement to him. She wasn't afraid he would dominate her. He was the most caring love of her life. She knew that she and her baby would be in the best of hands. To see her husband in the soil, making it possible for life to grow, made her heart swell with joy. Everything that bloomed in her yard was because of him. He would work that same way in raising their family. She was surrounded by flowers, citrus, and different plants. She was finally living her dream to be a writer. Kate discovered who she was, a woman who had her dreams come true with love. Kate was now complete, and it came about with patience and Garrett.

Garrett drove over to see his mother in the afternoon. He wanted to help her with some things at her home. Garrett expected this to be an emotional time. Mary had been going through Charles' things and sorted what she wanted to keep. She had called Garrett earlier to help her out.

"Mom, where are you?" Garrett called out.

"I'm in your dad's office." Her sadness was audible.

"Hey, Mom. You should have let me help you with this."

155

"It's okay. It's hard to be in here. Everything in this office was his. He had a special way of finding a place for his things. He even kept the pottery dish Callen made in the second grade for candy. I never even knew he saved it."

"Dad had secret feelings. I think he really wanted to be sensitive."

"He did. I boxed up some of the books he loved and some of the photographs he displayed on his shelf."

"What are those boxes in the kitchen?"

"His clothes. Rosy is going to come by and donate them for me. I kept a few of his shirts with the smell of his cologne. He saved a shirt I bought him when we went to Hawaii. He hated it but he wore it for me, and we took a picture together with him wearing it."

She began to cry in Garrett's arms.

"Oh, Mom. I know you still love him. I think it's good you want to keep some of his things."

"When does the pain go away? He was my only love. He was older and he was never married before me. I was the one he was waiting to give his love to." She looked up at Garrett, "Did you know he was artistic like you?"

"Dad? I never knew that about him."

"Let me show you something you would appreciate."

Mary went to a wooden box. Inside were special stones, pieces of carved wood, drawings, and petrified wood that he collected on different trips with Mary.

"This box was made by his grandfather. He gave it to him before he died. He used to draw these little landscapes when we used to go hiking in our younger days. He loved trees too."

"Why didn't he ever show me these?"

"He felt they were menial and not important to anyone but him. He used to find wooden pieces that looked unusual or just had something the other pieces didn't have."

"Mom, these are nice!"

In the box was a photo of Charles and his grandfather Sam. They used to go fishing and crabbing together. Charles' own father avoided spending time with him. Charles' grew up thinking of his grandfather as Dad. He would tell him stories about his life, the loves he treasured, and how much fishing relaxed him. He was a crafted fly fisherman, teaching Charles everything from the best way to cast, to bringing home a catch. He loved him very much. Saving these things helped him remember those good times they had when he was younger.

"Garrett, did I ever tell you the story about how your father and I met?"

"No, I don't think you did. Do you want to tell me now?"

"We met at a picnic the neighbors were having. My family just moved into the area. Charles couldn't stop looking at me. He must have thought I was cute or something. It made him nervous to think of talking to me, I could tell by the expression on his face. He was older, so maybe he thought, "Why would she want to talk to me when there are other young guys she could have?" I was wearing pearls around my neck. As I walked past Charles, the clasp broke somehow, and it fell on the ground. I had trouble with it before the picnic. Anyhow, your dad took the opportunity to pick it up for me. I smiled at him, and I was drawn to him. He asked to sit with me while we ate. I loved and enjoyed his company. I was wearing a seersucker pink dress that day and I felt like a schoolgirl talking to him. We really enjoyed being together. He had the most amazing laugh. I liked that he was older, and he was shy, kind of like you were. He was an only child and not having the affection of a father he felt uneasy around strangers. With my company, he adjusted right away, not second guessing his affections."

"Amazing. I wish I knew about this when he was alive."

"He only shared that with me. He had a quiet side, but that was his father's fault. He didn't have much of a mother to care for him either. Losing his granddad was sad for him."

"I'm beginning to understand Dad more. I wish Callen could know this about him."

"Give your brother time. It was a rocky relationship with those two. Callen will learn in his own time."

"Thank you for showing me these. I hope my child loves landscapes as much as us."

"That will be a joy to see."

Mary could see some of her husband in each of her children. The healing process was going to take more time. Her happiness came from those in her family who loved and supported her as a mother. Garrett felt it was a good time to talk about what she was going to do about her house.

"What did you and Becky decide about your house? Are you going to sell it?"

"She left it up to me. I'm not sure I can take care of this place by myself. Sam's not going to do it. I would have to hire out your landscapers to keep the place up. It just seems so big."

"Where would you move to if you did sell?"

"Becky suggested I move to Rhode Island to be near her. But I turned her down. I love it here in Santa Barbara. My family is here. Maybe I should keep the house for a while until I know what I want to do."

"I think you will know what to do. If you need anything, I'll be around. Let me know."

"I love you, son. You are a big help. Thank you."

Garrett would always care for Mary. He knew she was going to have to sell their family home to simplify her life with Sam.

Callen wasn't ready to visit her at her home. Mary thought about what she could do or say to help him adjust to losing his father. Callen needed his mother's caring love to heal his broken heart and was very fortunate to have her in his life. She was the one who kept them all together.

After Garrett went home to Kate, the house suddenly felt empty to Mary. Looking around, she remembered when all the boys lived at home. The house used to be filled with noise and movement. A family once lived there. It made her think about what Garrett said about selling the house. Each day she woke up, it was a genuine surprise not to see Charles in the kitchen with his morning coffee and paper. She at times expected him to come shave in the bathroom while she was trying to get ready. His things had been cleared and out of the way. Not much but a trace of him was in the home except a few pictures of him with his family and their wedding picture. She would come into the kitchen and see the chair he used to sit in. Before he died, he had a shirt resting on his office chair and she just couldn't remove it. It still held the smell of his after shave. She touched the walls, wrapped her arms around his suits, holding them tight as she cried out his name.

The boxes that were packed with Charles' clothes were picked up by the donation station Rosy volunteered for. It was hard for Mary to see them go. All the other things were going to go in a special trunk Mary had before marrying Charles. She too had treasures she kept; keepsakes her husband gave her. There were special cards and tissue paper with dried flowers from their anniversary. She wore the diamond ring he gave her when they had Garrett. She would always carry him with her in heart. Those changes were difficult, but Mary would learn to lean on those memories of the two of them.

She was tired of purging her pain. She wanted to be over this. After those months, she needed her grieving complete in order to take care of Sam. She would always be in love even though he was gone. She built a strong bond in her marriage that no one would ever replace. She refused to think about getting married again. No one knew Charles like Mary did. A love that was complicated at times but rewarding filled her with tenderness and a giving spirit. Mary was forever grateful for the chance to be loved by the greatest man with a difficult childhood but learned how to love Mary Jean Carrington.

# Chapter 18

The time came when Kate gave birth to a daughter. They named her Katelyn Dayne Carrington. She was beautiful in the eyes of her parents. That was the day they prayed would come after they lost their first pregnancy. Kate was glowing as a new mother. The community brought flowers, cards, gifts, and balloons to the new family. Giving birth at home was so comfortable for Kate. Garrett was very supportive and patient. He stayed by her side during the delivery and watched her nurse baby for the first time. They were both on a cloud.

Mary stopped by to see her first grandchild. Rosy wanted to give Kate a shower and thought of so many things to plan. Garrett had his family there to share in the moment, except for Callen. He tried to call him, but he didn't want to talk. It was obvious the crush from his father's death was still causing pain and anxiety. After the guests left, Garrett wanted to visit his brother.

"Where are you going?" Kate asked.

"I'm going to go see Callen for a short time. He's not talking to anyone right now. Something's wrong."

"Wait, wait. Don't go. It seems every time it looks like he's in distress, you run to him. He has Cassie. I really think you should let them handle it."

"Kate, I can't do that. This was a blow to Callen. I know he's suppressing his emotions. I'm sorry, but I have to go to him."

"Garrett, I need you here, please..."

"Let me do this. I'll be right back."

Before Garrett arrived, Cassie was trying to talk with him. He had been isolating himself and not wanting to be around anything that would trigger him.

"Callen, it's been days since we had a conversation. Honey, what are you feeling?" Cassie begged.

"I think you would have known by now. My father is dead."

"I know. I'm not expecting you to get over it soon, but..."

"But what? Is that what you want? You want me to get over it? Well, I can't do that. All my life I wanted him to be there for me and he wasn't!" Callen was shouting.

"Cal, please don't yell at me. I want my husband back."

"I don't want to be anything to you."

"You don't mean that."

Callen lowered his voice, "Yes, I do. You had it all. You had a father who loved you. You could talk about anything that was on your mind. I never had that! We didn't finish what we were trying to fix. And now he's gone."

"Maybe my situation is different. But I too lost a dad. He's gone too. You think I don't still grieve? Do you think just because I laugh I don't hurt like you do? Everyone is different. We all grieve differently. I love you because you helped fill that emptiness and all I was thinking about was the good times. How dare you throw that in my face!" Cassie grabbed her bag to leave.

163

"Where are you going?"

"I'm going to my mother's for the evening. You can sit here and grieve by yourself."

As she left, Callen sat on the couch holding his head in his hands. His crying was painful and at that instant, he picked up a glass and threw it against the wall. He was sobbing, deep inside missing his father. He felt bad that he took out his sadness on Cassie. Callen could hear Garrett's pickup truck pull in.

"Callen. Callen, it's Garrett. I know you're home. Open the door."

"Go away, Garrett."

"Callen, open the door. Can I talk to Cassie?"

"She's not here."

"Just open the door. Please, open it."

Garrett had his head against the door, resting his fist on the knob. He was begging and hoping he would listen. Garrett loved Callen and wanted to be the brother to help him through his process. Suddenly, the door opened slightly.

"Thank you."

"What do you want?"

"I wanted you to see Kate and our baby. What happened here?" as he noticed the broken pieces on the floor.

"I got angry when Cassie left. She's staying at her mother's."

164

"Why?"

"Her father died too, but I told her his passing wasn't the same as mine. She got mad and walked out."

"How could you say that to her?"

"Her dad loved her. He was a good man to her."

"That shouldn't make a difference. She is still missing him just like you miss our Dad. How could you demean her feelings like that?"

"I don't want to have this talk with you."

"I would never talk to Kate that way. We've all been through loss, you're not the only victim. You are going to have to get help. Can you talk to your therapist about this?"

"That's not going to bring him back, Garrett!"

"I know it won't. But you have too much pain. Do you want to go see Mom?"

"I can't go to that house."

"I want you to. See your mother. She needs you. She is feeling the sadness too."

"What if I can't?"

"I think you can. I know you hate feeling this way. We said our goodbyes to Dad. Don't say that to our mom."

Callen kneeled beside his brother and held him.

"I miss him, Garrett. I miss him. It's not fair! I really loved him," Callen cried.

"I miss him too. I got you, Brother. I got you."

The brothers cried together for the first time after his death. Losing their father moved that mountain. Tears, and the pain of losing the one they loved was real, and they needed each other to cope.

"Do you think you could drop me off at Cassie's mother's home?"

"Anything for you, Cal."

Callen felt awkward knocking on their door.

Cassie's mother answered, "Hello, Callen. Did you want to speak to your wife?"

"Yes." She came through the door and walked outside next to Callen.

"What are you doing here? I'm not sure I want to talk to you."

"I saw Garrett today. I'm sorry for what I said to you. Losing your father was hard. Probably just as hard as mine. I was just angry about not having closure with him before he died."

"I can understand your pain. But you did have that. He loved you, he moved on from it and wanted you in his life again. He died and took that with him. I'm sure he had closure. You and me? We have to talk to each other in a manner that helps us go on so we can heal together. Can you do that with me?"

"I'm going to try. I know my problems are not your fault. I keep getting these waves of anxiety that are impossible to live through. I won't hurt you like that again."

166

"Where are you going to go from here? You know I am okay with you going to see the therapist. Will you?"

"I'll do it for you, Cassie."

"No, do it for the both of us. I love you and I need you in my life. It's important because we are going to have a baby."

Callen was so surprised that he took Cassie in his arms and spun her around and kissed her. This news was a new beginning for this family and for Callen.

"How long have you known?" Callen asked.

"A few weeks. I didn't want to tell you because I know you were too sad. I didn't know how you would feel about it."

"I feel wonderful. A baby for us. This makes me happy."

"Can we go home now?" Cassie asked.

Callen knew that meeting with his mother was important. He was nervous about being in the house where his father died. To walk into that house where he used to be would leave an emptiness in his heart. It was crucial that he talk to his mother about how he felt about missing his father.

Sam meant everything to him as well. He wanted a strong relationship with his younger brother to help him grow up without resentment. Callen would be there for his brother after getting help with his moods and anxiety.

After pulling in the driveway, he stayed in the car pondering. He was preparing himself to walk in the house he grew up in and not see Charles. He had to think about Cassie and his baby and what Garrett, and his family meant to him. He thought about Kate, how she was the best thing that came into his life. She was the one who helped him see his potential to do well for himself. She saw how a divided family was still able to stand up to anything it went through. She had a part in mending by giving the best of herself. Callen finally climbed out of the car to challenge his emotions.

"Callen, honey it's good to see you," Mary reassured.

"Hi, Mom. I wanted to see how you're feeling."

"I'm better. I had to make a few changes around the house to make it feel more comfortable for me and Sam. I still think your father will be home soon, and he is still here at times."

"Yeah, I get that. I felt nervous coming here."

"Why? This was your home."

"Because Dad died here. I miss him so much."

"I do too. I emptied the office and put some of his things away. Do you remember that box he had that you asked me about? I was going through it, and I found a letter. It was in this envelope with your name on it from Dad."

Callen took the letter and started to open it.

"Son, you can read it in private if you want to."

"No, I think we should read it together. I think you should hear it."

"Alright, Callen. You can read it aloud."

Callen could feel the tears coming as he unfolded it. He never thought his father would write anything about their relationship. These were his last words to Callen.

*My Son Callen,*

    *I have never been able to write the right words and tell you how I feel about you. When my grandfather died, I felt lost. He was my dad in my heart. My father couldn't care for me or my mother. He was too broken of a man to give love. He tried, but he was miserable and died young. We never had a conversation before he died. I never got to tell him how I loved him or what he meant to me. He just went away. I cried for weeks, losing my dad and grandfather. They both died of heart disease, and I knew eventually I would succumb to the disease as well. When I was young, I was diagnosed with a defective heart. I was treated for it, and I only told your mother about how afraid I was to die and leave my family. Then I had a heart attack. I was able to see my sons get married. I wanted to let you know, Callen, that I love you very much. I should have been a better father, but I was much like my dad. I tried to be like my grandfather who taught me all he knew. He saved my life and made the future look good for me. Then I met your mother and I just wanted all of you to be happy. I haven't been feeling well. I am having chest pains and becoming tired. I don't know how long I have, and you should know that when we last spoke, I heard every word. I forgive anything that was said out of turn and want you to forgive me too. I know, I should just say this to you. I want you to be happy, my son. I almost lost someone who I dearly loved and admired, you. You came back from pain and heartbreak, and I want to be part of your healing process. I keep this letter safe until I am brave enough to give it to your mother. I wanted to call you and have her give it to you. You can call me or come by after you read it. I can't wait to see my son who has grown into a fine husband. All my love, Dad.*

Mary held on to Callen's hand while he read the letter. He shed tears, hearing his father's words with true and pure love. He finally realized the closure he needed. Callen walked around the house noticing how different it felt. He was emotional, yet happy his father truly loved him.

"Thank you for giving this to me, Mom. I'm grateful to have had a dad like him."

Callen looked around. It felt lonely in the house.

"Wow, there's a lot of things packed up. Where is everything?"

"Some of it is packed up in storage. After giving it deep consideration, I've decided to sell this old house."

"I'm stunned you want to sell it. Are you sure you want to do that?"

"I can't keep living here without your father. Sam needs me and I want to be happy for him, and for you.

"You have to do what makes you feel better. Selling the house might help but it won't fix everything."

"I know, but I have made up my mind and I think it's the right thing to do."

Callen hugged his mother. He supported what she knew was best for her and Sam. He took the letter and turned to look at his father's office one more time.

"I love you, Dad," he whispered.

He turned after shutting the door. He had to walk around the house and look into the rooms remembering his shared room with Garrett, the kitchen where they had family meals, and where Charles sat. The good memories flooded his mind as he prepared to say goodbye to the home he will always cherish with his family.

He thought of Cassie and how he was now going to share his life with her and their new child. He would be an exceptional father, a father who would love his children for all time.

Mary would see Charles' legacy carry on in her family. It was their dream to have grandchildren running around their house. They would hear stories about their grandfather and the love he had in his heart. Callen would help his mother make arrangements to figure on a sale price and finalize everything so she could move on. Love grew up in this house. No matter what storm came through that home, love conquered each one and a loving family survived...together

# Chapter 19

The months went by, and the babies were growing up. Mary laughed and played with her granddaughters, Katelyn and Cassidy. The curls of gold and adoring giggles gave her a warm sense of home. Bib overalls and laced socks topped off their ensemble. That was where Mary needed to be, among those who gave her the most deserved life from the family she started with Charles.

Mary finally sold her home and bought a smaller one near Callen and his family where Sam could be closer to him. Before Mary closed the sale of her home, she and Sam took a moment to say goodbye. Sam, of course, was going to miss the pool. Mary walked around, touching her kitchen countertop, looking out the window where she washed dishes, revisiting the bedroom she shared with Charles, and reliving all the memories. She took one last look before closing the door. With her bags packed, she and Sam were ready to start a new chapter of life together.

Weeks later, Kate stopped by to see her mother.

"I came as quickly as I could. What is wrong with Aunt Karen's house?"

"Nothing. I had a real estate developer pay me a visit. He wanted to buy my house. His mother knew Karen and he saw pictures of this beautiful, historic home."

"Please tell me you didn't sell it to him!"

"I did not sell the house. He did offer me a lot of money for it. You know this is our home. I promised my sister I would keep it in the family."

"It doesn't matter how long Karen has been gone, over the years, this house has been a big part of my life."

"We do have so many memories here," reminisced Maddy.

"Moving to Santa Barbara changed who I used to be. I don't want to think of where we would be if we never moved here."

"It's been a while since Daryl left, Kate. How are you feeling about him these days?"

"I feel stronger. To know that I will always love my family. I'm glad he never came back."

"It was hard for the boys when he didn't call or write, but they knew we would be happy regardless of who he proved himself to be."

Maddy became close friends with Mary. Sharing grandchildren and both losing husbands, they became loyal friends during their adjustment to life.

"I love Mary's new house. Have you seen it? I went to see her last week. She just can't get enough of those grandkids."

"They really love her. Do you ever think she will remarry someday?" Kate inquired.

"Well, that's up to her. We are close, so I believe she will love spending her years on her own. She loved Charles too much."

"We all still miss him."

"That will never go away. The kind of love they had was special. Mary made everything better for Charles. He was more than proud of his wife for being a good partner."

Kate knew she had the same confidence in Garrett as Mary had with Charles. Kate never felt judged by him even though there were times she became adamant about her opinions. She was strong-willed and Garrett appreciated her for that.

Maddy cherished the relationship she had with Kate. She went through the tough times with Kate, never giving up on what she knew she would become; a woman who was truly loved. It was good to see her standing on her own.

"I have something to show you. I think you'll like this," said Maddy.

Maddy took Kate upstairs and showed her a rolled up piece of blueprint.

"Where did you get this?" Kate asked surprised.

"The realtor gave me the blueprints to Karen's house when it was built. Look at the date, 1925."

"This is amazing that you have it."

"Kate, there is a special place in my heart for this house. It saved our lives. It gave me the peace to deal with what your father put us through. We persevered and we survived."

"I wish I could get those years back, take back my frustration. I couldn't see that we were going to be okay. Who

I am now is not who I was then. I wish I could have grown up in this house."

"You did grow up here. Emotionally it shaped you into the woman you are today. Karen's love, our endurance and closeness, shaped you. There is no need to look back on your past because you made a good life for yourself."

"You did good too, Mom."

For these women there was no reason to look back. The trials they went through and the love they had for the Carrington family bonded their closeness as the seasons changed throughout the years. Could this family have been healed without the help of Kate? Maybe, but her devotion and choices gave her the courage to help close the gap between brothers and family who were sadly divided. Their forgiveness gave them back their father who realized his past should not prevent showing love. Charles would always be remembered as a father, who in his heart, loved his family. He was no longer judged but honored.

Maddy chose to find love in her friends and family. She worked hard to protect her heart. She was remembered for her florist shop for thirty-seven years. Everyone she met felt like family. She was all about family; she was all about love.

Callen burned his cane during a family gathering. He told his story about scars and his accident to his children. His promise to them was that he would always be there, to help them make choices to protect them from harmful consequences. He shared his story about his father, how they amended their relationship that turned to love.

175

Callen's children meant the world to him. As a father and husband, he became the person he always wanted to be. He was a math teacher who was thankful for making a better choice. He was also in love, with a history teacher who supported and praised him for all his effort to become happy again. His true love gave him  courage to manage anxieties and enjoy his life.

Garrett would always love landscaping. Retired now, he went on to train younger landscapers to love the art of living things in the soils of life. Everything he taught came from his love of natural things. He was thankful that he waited until his true love came into his life, his Kate. She became a nurturing mother and caring wife. Garrett saw her good heart despite heartaches. He could see who she really was.

Kate became a popular author and was listed on the Best Seller's List many times, writing inspiring romance stories and poems that filled the soul with positive hope. Kate continued to write into her retirement years. Her fanbase couldn't get enough of her motivating and encouraging prose. She washed away the doubts about herself. Her experiences had helped her write beautifully, settled into a life with Garrett, choosing to pass on her wisdom to her children and grandchildren.

# Chapter 20

The past was gone. New memories would surface, the good and the bad times would continue to strengthen the family and remind them to rely on each other. Who would have thought that the young girl from a concrete city could see her life blossom into a garden of hope and love?

As she sits with her husband on their porch, she reflects on how their love set the stage for where she is today. She is among mature trees, flowers, and all that nurtures her.

"It has been thirty-eight years since I heard my mother's words, "You will get your reward." Nothing had a greater impact on me than those words. Garrett, I miss her so much," Kate recalls.

"She lived a full life, Kate. You are the image of your mother, inside your heart. She lived her life seeing you become a happy daughter," Garrett smiles.

"I love how our mothers helped us get to where we are. It is hard to imagine that they are both gone."

"Kate, my Kate," he reached for her hand. "Over the years, I continue to fall in love with you. Each year you are more beautiful to me. Thank you for being my best friend, my love. Who knew that being married to a landscaper would look so good on you?"

"I remember when I wanted to be in your arms forever. I know we are older now and we never missed a chance to see where life has taken us. I love how our family has grown."

"We are a blessed family. Old, but blessed."

"Do you want to see something? The Historical Society sent over the final photographs for the article I'm writing for Karen's house."

"I can't believe it's being honored like this. After your mother died, I knew you wanted it to be preserved."

"I think the community would love to walk through those rooms to see how beautiful my aunt and mother kept it. I know when I visit, it brings me to tears. Oh, how much I loved that house."

"I'm happy you're keeping it in the family."

"I designed the plaque that is going on the front of the house."

"Show me what you designed."

She unfolded a page and read,

> *This house became a home to Karen and Michael Baier. Built in 1925 and restored to its natural beauty. We dedicate this home to Madeline Parker, the sister of Karen, who filled this place with love and warmth. Cherished memories were created here. May everyone who comes into this house enjoy the beauty and history within its walls.*
>
> *Katharine Victoria Carrington*

*The Landscaper's Wife*

*Annette Stephenson*

Made in the USA
Monee, IL
24 June 2022

98457287R00105